Hatchet Sisters

Coffin Kids

By

Bryan Higby Rick Snyder

The DenMark Chronicles

CW01497682

All characters and events in this novel are fictional and not to be taken literally.

This book is dedicated to the original Death Strides
– Barb, Patti and Tammy

Prologue

There was something about the alleys in DenMark. Things happened in those alleys. Take this scene - A small child coming home from school on a late autumn day, a Friday, which was just about the best day of the week for kids. Friday after the bell rang meant freedom for a whole two days. Two days to do whatever a nine-year-old girl wanted to do. This little girl, Margie Miles, raced down the street stopping in front of The Golden Dawn Chinese restaurant on Cobb Street.

She stared down the alley next to the restaurant. The alley was dark. Dark and filled with shadows. These were the places inside the city that her older brother James told her to keep clear of. He said they were scary places, forgotten places. Bad people lurked inside those places. Margie promised that she would never go into a place like that, *never*.

But it was Friday and school was out, and besides, the sky was blue and the sun was shining. Most of the shadows in the alley were still tiny, barely noticeable. Also, running through this alley would get her home ten minutes sooner than going her normal route. Cutting through the alley would also allow her to stay away from that creepy place on Bradbury Street. The old Winkie Witch house was nothing but rubble now, burned a year before, but she and her friends claimed the witch's evil spirit still lurked inside the ruins.

Margie looked up and down Cobb Street. It was bustling with happy Friday people. They were getting out of work and school. The world was good. She would make the trip down the alley to the other end quick. Margie happened to know that her mother had bought the ingredients to make a batch of oatmeal and raisin cookies, her favorite. Her mother knew how Margie liked to lick the spoon when they finished. The young girl tightened her book bag over her shoulders and sprinted down the alley. When she saw the shadow from the corner of her eye she froze.

"Ah!" Margie cried, looking as the small shadow pounced from behind a dumpster.

A cat, it had to be a stray cat, they were always lurking outside of Chinese restaurants. She laughed at that joke – cats and Chinese restaurants went together like white on rice, that's what her brother James always said.

Margie started forward again but when the shadow moved closer to her she hesitated looking back.

"Why...why, you're not a cat at all...you're a, *monkey*?"

Margie watched as the shadow manifested as a colorfully dressed monkey. She couldn't believe what she was looking at. A monkey in a clown suit? Couldn't be, could it? Maybe there was a circus in town? She hadn't heard of anything, but maybe.

"Hi there. My name's Margie. What's yours?"

She didn't actually expect the monkey to speak, but when it did she stood mouth agape.

"Roscoe! My name's Roscoe," the monkey said. His voice was low and guttural, much older sounding than he looked.

"Wow! Can you actually speak?"

"Yeah, can't you?"

The monkey looked different now. The more it spoke the uglier it became.

"I uh, I have to go," Margie said as she tried to walk past the monkey.

When it stepped in front of her the girl stopped, feeling an unaccustomed fear run up her spine. Margie's brother was correct; she should never have come down this alley. Margie turned to sprint back to the street but two figures stepped out from behind the dumpster.

"Oh! Thank gosh. There's a monkey..." Margie said turning then only to see that the monkey had vanished.

The two figures stepped closer to her. Margie noticed quickly that the figures were a couple of girls a little older than her and they were wearing summer dresses, but it was autumn, and chilly despite the sun.

"Hello, my name's Margie Miles, who are you?"

When she saw the hatchet in their hands her eyes went huge and she screamed…

Chapter One

James sat listening to his mother scream and his father blubber as the cop talked to them about his younger sister Margie's death. Her body was found mutilated in an alley. The cop, thank God, did not go into details but he did request James's parents to accompany him in the cruiser to the local police precinct to identify the body.

James was fifteen years old and fine to stay on his own. He made it clear that he had no intension on going to identify his nine-year-old sister's body.

When they left James went into Margie's bedroom and laid down on her bed. He could smell her pristine fragrance. James had teased his sister over the years, just the way kids do, but he regretted it now and would for the rest of his life. Someone had killed her. Having a murdered sister wasn't like she died of cancer or got run over, as horrible as that sounded. No, having her *murdered* was worse. It was like the cosmos opened and hacked her up just out of spite. James was torn up because *he* was the one to tell Margie never to go down a dark alley in DenMark. Could this warning have opened his sister to the cosmos targeting her?

James brushed the burning tears from his eyes for a minute and punched the pillows on his sister's bed. He wanted to die now. His sister was dead and he had no more siblings. His parents were too old to try again. James would never be able to attend his little sister's graduation, or her wedding. Those future memories were wiped out by some madman's rage. James punched the pillow again promising that he would find this crazy killer and make him pay for what he had done to Margie. No matter what the cost, he would pay.

#

Horatio walked past the Impossible Dreams Thrift Store every day on his way to school. He had graduated from Harper Elementary to Barker Middle School where Rachel Brooks attended. Rachel was Horatio's one and only genuine crush. With her beautiful red hair and green eyes she just knocked his socks off every time he saw her. Of course since the events at the Winkie Witch House over a year ago he had seen less and less of Rachel.

He was thinking about Rachel Brooks when he heard someone calling to him.

"Hey, Fat Kid!"

It was Charlie Bokar, one of the Bokar twins. Charlie had the head of hair bright as the sun. His brother Henry's hair was dark as midnight. They were closer than two twins could be. They were also present during the destruction of the Winkie Witch's House on Bradbury Street.

"Hey Chuck, where's Henry?"

"He stayed after school again, helpin' out some teacher. Wanta go with me to The Dreams?"

'The Dreams' in Charlie Bokar language referred to the Impossible Dreams Thrift Store that Horatio was currently passing.

"Ah, no thanks Chuck, I gotta get home and help my mom with dinner. Dad's away and she could use the help," Horatio said ducking his head and hunching his shoulders.

"Suit yourself, but old Tom's got some killer new stuff. If you know what I mean?"

Horatio knew what Charlie meant. The Impossible Dreams Thrift Store wasn't like other thrift stores, it wasn't like any stores at all. That place was an oasis for magic - white, black, you name it. He and the others, Rachel, Henry, and Charlie, had taken a taste of that magic a year ago when they battled DenMark's resident witch – Winkie Foote. She had been kidnapping kids and eating them, just like the Grimms' fairytales mentioned. There were taffy clowns too.

"Stop," Horatio told himself as he watched Charlie Bokar skip down the rutty walkway to the front of the thrift store.

He didn't want to think about those events last year, he couldn't. He had almost died then, they all had. They were a close-knitted unit then. Horatio wore a super hero suit, Henry was a zombie, Charlie a werewolf, and Rachel Brooks was a mistress of the night. It was those masks and outfits that changed them into their respective roles. That magic derived from inside the Impossible Dreams. Magic, Horatio found, was addictive. The stitching that had kept them so tight as a group had frayed over the year since last Halloween. Now they were barely acquaintances.

Fat Kid watched as Charlie Bokar entered the grimy front door of the thrift store. He was envious of the boy. Horatio did want to go inside the thrift store and the story he told about helping his mother with dinner was nothing but a lie. Since his father had left on the recent logging contract his mother spent most of her time zoned out on the couch watching game shows and soap operas. Horatio had to eat frozen dinners. Many nights he had to heat up dinner for her. The boy hated when his father was away. He preferred his father's chili, or homemade chicken soup with big chunks of meat, to the frozen dinners.

Horatio turned away from the Impossible Dreams and started home. When he reached the Chinese restaurant, The Golden Dawn on Cobb Street, he saw the alley that he normally crossed to get home was blocked off with yellow and black police tape. The alley was empty. No police. Horatio glanced down the street and noticed a Chinese kid exiting the front of the restaurant with a delivery. He was wearing a helmet and was approaching a moped.

"Hey, excuse me," Horatio called to the kid on the moped.

The kid looked up.

"Yeah?"

"What happened in here?" Fat Kid motioned toward the alley.

"Oh, terrible, some little girl got axed there on Friday afternoon," the Chinese kid said shaking his head as he started his moped and sped off.

Fat Kid stared down the shadowy alley. It was only a little after three p.m.. but the alley seemed darker than it should have. The shadows were deep and unmoving, or were they…

He heard the kid crying next to him and Horatio almost jumped.

To his left stood a teenager, blonde hair, and freckled faced. The kid was looking into the alley and crying like mad. Horatio watched the boy for a second or two and then started past him when the kid spoke.

"I warned her you know. I told her - *stay out of the alleys*," the kid said.

He wiped a gob of snot off the end of his nose and then looked at Fat Kid. The kid's eyes were red as red could be. Horatio didn't think he ever saw anyone that miserable and hoped he never would again.

"I'm gonna find them, whoever did this to my sister…I'm gonna find them and they'll be sorry," the kid said and then stormed off.

Horatio watched the poor kid. Fat Kid was really missing his old man now. A little girl gets killed in an alley? Horatio glanced back toward the Impossible Dreams Thrift Store and wondered if the magic inside had leaked out, the horrible black magic that he knew existed there.

Again Horatio dismissed the idea of tripping back to the thrift store in favor of going home. He propped up his jacket collar, the afternoon had become chilly, and headed home taking the long way around.

Chapter Two

They were pervs she heard. Nick and Fish were
a couple of holdouts from a by-gone era where
dudes hung around in drug stores and convenient
stores drinking coffee and smoking cigarettes. Nick
looked a bit more respectable with his white dress
shirt and tie, while Fish, well Fish was strictly
grunge.

"Horrible to hear about that little girl," Nick
said.

He was speaking not with Fish but with the
cashier, a guy named Frank.

"Yeah. Not surprised though. Kids these days,"
Frank said.

"Kids these days," Fish echoed Frank's
sentiment but there was a slight scorn in Fish's
scruffy delivery.

Rachel listened to this exchange with curious
ears as a red-haired kid bumped into her.

"Watch it," she said.

When she noticed that the red head was
sticking beef jerky into his pockets she looked over
at Frank, the cashier. Frank seemed to have lost

interest in the conversation with his loiterers, Nick and Fish, and was reading the horse track racing forms. Rachel looked back at the red head kid. She had seen him around school.

"Hey, you're Roy right?"

He looked up at her and his upper lip peeled back in a snarl. The kid had to be like fourteen pushing twenty. She could see the shadow of red facial hair on his freckled face and Roy was still in middle school.

"What's it to you," Roy said.

"Nothing," Rachel said but her green eyes fell to the beef jerky the kid was stealing.

"You want some?"

Roy seemed to honestly be asking her, like maybe he was doing her a favor.

"No thanks," Rachel said pulling out a five dollar bill that she pilfered from her mother's coffee can atop the refrigerator at home. "I could pay for those if you want me to."

She was whispering now. She saw Roy's face soften and he actually wasn't a bad looking pre-teen, but as quick as the expression softened it hardened again and he strutted past her and out the front door like he owned the place. Rachel shook her head, bought her gallon of milk that she had come for, and then left.

#

Outside Rachel saw Henry Bokar walking down the street with his head lowered, a book in the crook of his elbow. On his own Henry Bokar got bullied a lot. Of course when he was with his twin, Charlie, no one dared bully the two of them together. They were smarter than almost any teenager or adult, and fast too.

Rachel looked around but did not see Charlie.

"Hey Hank. Where's Chuck?"

Henry Bokar glanced up surprised that there was a friendly in the neighborhood.

"Oh, hi Brooks. Chuck? The Dreams'd be my guess. That's where I'm headed as well."

He started forward.

"You see Horatio around?"

Henry stopped and turned back.

"Fat Kid? Nah, not since the summer. Seen him at the drive-in's a couple of times with his folks," Henry said.

He seemed anxious to be off.

"You see Tom lately?"

"Almost every day. Me and Chuck visit the Dreams most afternoons. Tom throws us a little…"

"*Turn*?"

Henry seemed to brighten at that. He actually smiled.

"Yeah, a *turn*. Anyway, Chuck's probably there now. I'm gonna see. Wanta come?"

Rachel looked off thinking all that awaited her back at the trailer was her mother and maybe one of her mother's beaus. She lifted the gallon of milk over her shoulder and smiled.

"Lead the way, oh Henry Bokar."

Henry smiled as he turned on his heels and started down the street.

#

The inside of the Impossible Dreams Thrift Store was as cluttered as usual. Tom's ashtrays had doubled since Rachel had last been inside the shop. The old manager was chewing on a cigar arguing with Henry Bokar's blonde-haired brother, Charlie, as she and Hank entered.

"Hank would you tell this old geezer…" Charlie broke off when he saw Rachel Brooks enter. "Well, well."

Charlie seemed overly enthused to see Rachel. Rachel cocked and eyebrow and stared down at the blonde Bokar brother. They were both short for their age, ten, and Rachel was a tall twelve-year-old.

"Well, what?" Rachel asked.

"Nothing! Nothing. Nice to see ya legs," Charlie winked at her.

"Rachel," Tom said tipping the brim of his beat-up old brown Fedora.

"What were you guys talking about?" Henry asked.

"Nothing, nothing," Charlie and Tom said together.

Their expressions resembled a fox in henhouse caught by a farmer holding a shotgun. Henry and

16

Rachel immediately knew that Tom and Charlie had been scheming.

"Spill it," Rachel said.

Charlie and Tom exchanged a look and then Tom dropped a newspaper, The DenMark Gazette, onto the grimy glass counter and pointed at the headline – CHILD SLAIN IN ALLEY! The headline was in bright red ink that came off on Rachel's thumbs. She looked at her thumbs. They were as red as blood.

"I heard about this. What's it got to do with your dopey expressions?"

Rachel pushed the Gazette back across the counter not wanting to touch it again, as if maybe it possessed some black magic that would bring the slayer to her.

"Read how the poor child died," Tom said pushing the newspaper back toward Rachel and Henry.

They both read the cause of death.

"Hatchet, and she was only nine?"

A chill ran over Rachel's skin.

"Exactly. Now follow me," Tom said as he stuck his soggy cigar behind his left ear.

He led them down an aisle to a glass case with an empty display. There was a holder inside as if something that belonged in there was missing. Tom and Charlie watched Henry and Rachel look over the display.

"Something's missing," Henry said.

"No kidding Sherlock," Charlie said.

Henry pushed his brother, his brother pushed back.

"It was a hatchet?" Rachel asked.

Tom nodded.

"Old Charles here was doing inventory yesterday and noticed that the Borden Hatchet had gone missing," Tom said.

"Borden Hatchet? As in…"

"Lizzie Borden," Charlie cut her off.

"So you think that someone stole your Lizzie Borden hatchet and killed this young girl? Who would do something like that?" Rachel said.

All three of them looked at Rachel now like maybe she was joking.

"You kidding, sister? This city is filled with creepazoids who would love that kind of dark magic," Charlie said.

"And that's *just* the creeps in *this* city," Tom put in.

"What's that mean?" Rachel asked.

"Little lady this blue globe we live on is kinda like a fragile egg. There are many creepy crawlies on the outside trying to break the shell. Those thingies are always beating at our door. The...*owners* of the Impossible Dreams usually keep the thingies out but occasionally there will be a crack in the shell. Hence Winkie Witch."

Tom exited the back of the shop and walked to the counter pointing at the picture of the dark alley in the newspaper.

"Hence the hatchet murder."

"If that's true we need to find the killer before anyone else..." Rachel said.

Henry cut her off.

"Look."

He pointed at the television screen where Tom had his old Zenith tuned to the racing scores, but now the six o'clock news flashed across the screen. Tom turned up the volume.

Another grizzly murder on the Southside of DenMark this evening. The police have issued a formal statement but this reporter has received a credible tip off from an anonymous source that the second murder was also in an alley with a hatchet. Police are not speculating on the connection but they have said that the second victim was also a child. A temporary curfew is in effect city wide for any child under the age of sixteen. Any child caught out after dark will have their parents fined five hundred dollars...

"That's larceny!" Charlie said.

"Shhh!" Everyone else snapped back.

Of course we'll keep you fully informed here at WDMK. I'm Bob Smiley. Good night.

Tom switched off the volume as they all stood stunned. Tom checked his watch.

"It's almost six-thirty. Street lights are coming on. You kids better git home before curfew," Tom said.

He started to shoo them out the front door.

"Shouldn't we talk about this first?" Rachel said but they were at the door now.

She, Henry, and Charlie all glanced out the grimy glass door into the growing shadowy world outside of the safety of the Impossible Dreams. Rachel was thinking about her hitching back to the trailer park. It would be too embarrassing to call her mother just to hear Ilene Brooks complain about how her daughter was inconveniencing her, or worse, to hear her mother slurring drunk.

"Tom, you think you might give us a ride?"

"I would darling 'cept the Olds is under the weather. Heck it's on blocks right now," Tom said.

"No worries, Brooks," Charlie said removing a cell phone from his pocket.

"Hey where'd you get that Chuck?"

Henry was staring angrily at his brother. Charlie just shrugged and he hit speed dial.

"Yeah, Fish my man. Need a ride…Impossible Dreams," Charlie said and then he turned his back on the group and whispered into the cell phone before hanging up. "We got a ride."

"Yeah, who?"

Rachel seemed doubtful.

"Skeeter's Taxi. Got a guy named Fish," Charlie said smiling.

"Fish, you kidding? That guy's like a major perv and pot-head to boot Chuck, geez," Henry said disgusted.

"Maybe, but Fish has wheels and he's bona fide. He even has a real hack license. Got it last summer. He works for Skeeter's Taxi. Which reminds me. Brooks ya got any cash?"

"You kidding?"

She groaned removing the change she had left over from the milk. It was two dollars and fifty cents. Rachel held out the cash.

"I envy the coins being in those jeans," Charlie whispered to Henry. Henry pushed his brother and Rachel just smirked.

"Is it enough?"

"I don't know. To get way out to your place at the Industrial Park, Fish might have to take something out in exchange," Charlie joked.

"You're a jerk Chuck. Listen Brooks, if Fish needs more than two fifty we got cash back at our place. No worries," Henry said.

"My hero," Rachel leaned in kissing Henry and he went scarlet from his head to his toes. Charlie scowled at his brother's dumb luck.

It didn't take more than a couple of minutes for Fish to pull up to the street in front of the Impossible Dreams. The taxi was a clunky light-blue Caprice Classic spotted with rust and no rims. The Skeeter's Taxi sign was a magnet attached to only one side of the car and the light on top flickered as if there was a short circuit inside its socket.

"Nice wheels," Charlie said, leaning forward to open the door for Rachel.

Rachel stopped and looked back at Tom who was standing in the open door of the shop making sure they got safely inside the taxi.

"Tom, we'll talk about this later?"

"Yeah, old Tom's got a lot of work to do. Stop by tomorrow. While the sun's still shining," Tom said looking up into the darkening sky with an expression that pretty much said he wasn't sure if the sun would ever come up again.

Rachel took note of this expression as she heard the taxi horn blare for her to climb in. Henry and Charlie were already inside the taxi. She noticed how they elbowed each other to sit closer to her so Rachel slid into the front seat opposite Fish. Fish tossed his cigarette out the window where it sparked among the crisp downed leaves. Tom noticed the small spark and stepped on the embers. Fish smiled through the grimy window of the taxi and then sped off on bald tires.

#

The Winkie House on Bradbury Street had been truly horrible, but the news reports of the child butchering seemed somehow worse, more brutal. Horatio sat with the frozen dinner heated on his lumpy lap watching the six o'clock news report of the second child slaying. His mother lay on the couch snoring. A bottle of booze sat half empty on the end table next to a couple prescription pill bottles.

He was angry and scared, but the thing that hurt the worst was how lonely Horatio felt. A year ago when he, the Bokar Brothers, and Rachel teamed up to stop the Witch Winkie he felt like they had become a gang. He liked the three of them especially Rachel. His heart always skipped a beat when he thought of her. Horatio had barely seen her at school this year. Rachel Brooks seemed more like a ghost to him now. There were nights when he laid awake thinking about her and his super hero suit, the one old Tom gave him. The suit was locked away again in that old wooden footlocker at the Impossible Dreams.

"Horatio..." his mother slurred.

Fat Kid almost spilled his dinner when he heard his mother's voice.

"Mom?"

He was about to get off the couch when he realized that his mother was talking in her sleep. Horatio watched her roll over. She mumbled a couple of more things and was snoring again.

"Mom?" Horatio whispered.

He wasn't sure what the Impossible Dreams hours of operations were but Horatio Alger Patterson was itching to feel the fabric of that super suit again - just once more for old time's sake. The six o'clock news was ending. They covered almost nothing but the child slayer. If Horatio was still wearing that suit he would finish this crazy killer. He would keep this city safe from the evil like he had done with Winkie Witch.

Looking back down at his pathetic dinner tray and his thick stomach beneath made him lose his appetite.

Horatio carried the heated mashed potatoes, corn, and rubber steak into the kitchen where he dropped it into the trash. It was dark outside now. The streetlights were on. He had school in the morning, hump day, Wednesday. He had some more math homework to do. If he didn't finish for tomorrow he was in big trouble with his math teacher Mr. Stanley.

"So what," he mumbled.

Horatio dropped the lid to the trash can, snagged his jacket off the kitchen wall hook and exited out the back door.

The streets were almost completely deserted. He heard the news reporter, Bob Smiley, talking about a curfew at eight for all children under sixteen. Horatio was eleven now but he didn't care about this either, since it was only six forty-five. He had plenty of time kill.

Time to *kill*?

"Bad thoughts Fat Kid, bad thoughts," he whispered zipping up his jacket.

He would go to the Impossible Dreams and speak with Tom. He was sure that Tom would be willing to let Horatio have the super suit, for just one night. That's all he wanted, one more trip in the suit to save the city and be a hero. He needed this.

As Horatio started down Elm heading toward the intersection of Gotham and Bradbury he slowed feeling eyes watching him. The last time he felt this way it was on account of the Winkie Witch staring at him from the porch of her old Victorian house on Bradbury Street. But that house was nothing but ash now. Horatio reached the corner of Gotham and Bradbury. He stared down the street in the direction that he had to go in order to reach the Impossible Dreams Thrift Store.

Boy it was dark down there. The street lamps at that end of Bradbury were off. Shadows lurked at the end of the street and Horatio seriously considered taking the alley next to The Golden Dawn Chinese Restaurant. Then again, that's where the first child was...

"No! Stop it," Horatio said not wanting to think about the child slayer as he looked back at his own house.

The porch light was on and looked welcoming. But when Horatio thought about his father being away and his mother asleep on the couch he decided his initial idea to go to the Impossible Dreams was sound. He would just go there, meet with Tom, heck maybe even Charlie and Henry would be there. Smiling, Fat Kid stuck his hands into his pockets and moved quickly down the street.

By the time he reached the front of the ruined Winkie House Horatio had goose flesh running up and down his skin.

Almost there he was just about to walk past the burned remains of the old Winkie Witch's place then. He stared into the black abyss off to the right. The darkness appeared fuller, deeper and unclear. The street lights shown only up to the edge of the scorched fence and then ended. Looking back he could no longer see his house. He was more than halfway to the thrift store. There was no going back now.

"What was that old saying about whistling past the graveyard?" Horatio remembered them reading a story in school about a headless demon that chased a school teacher over a rickety bridge.

Horatio started to whistle as he skipped past the remains of the Winkie House. When he got to the other side he noticed that it was full dark outside. The stars had come out and the temperature had dropped a whole ten degrees. He wished that he had brought his heavier jacket now. The chilly October air was downright freezing.

"Just a little further," he said and he was right.

Wasn't that the gaudy neon lights of The Golden Dawn Chinese Restaurant up ahead? Sure it was, but boy it got strange on these DenMark streets after dark. It was easy to get turned around and lost. There wasn't even any fog but Fat Kid was frightened. As Horatio moved forward he realized that he had progressed from skipping to almost jogging. When he reached Cobb Street where the restaurant was he stopped, taking in deep gulps of breath. His gut heaved. Horatio wiped a thin layer of sweat off his forehead as he moved forward. He peered down the alley with the dumpster where the little Miles girl died.

He stopped when he felt something squishy beneath his sneaker. Lifting his foot he noticed some kind of excrement attached. He had stepped in dog poop, but...this didn't look like any dog poop he had ever seen before, and besides, DenMark citizens were supposed to clean up after their pets. It was the law.

"Yuck!" Horatio said smelling the rancid stink of the stuff.

What happened next was so bizarre that at first Horatio felt like maybe the walk here had frightened him silly. Standing just off the sidewalk in the shadow of the Cobb Street alley was a colorfully dressed monkey.

"A monkey? In DenMark," Horatio whispered.

Before he knew what was happening the monkey was doing some silly tricks, walking on its hands, doing somersaults. Horatio forgot his fear for a moment and actually laughed. The monkey was making him laugh for the first time in weeks, since his father went off on his latest logging trip.

"Hi there, silly one. What's your name?" Horatio asked.

"Roscoe, what's yours?"

Fat Kid stopped smiling as he heard the deep guttural voice coming out of the monkey. The boy's eyes went wide and he made sure to stay on the sidewalk and out of the dark alley. Then he glanced down at the monkey poop on his sneaker as the monkey, Roscoe, cackled its pleasure.

"Disgusting," Horatio said.

"Disgusting," Roscoe said scornfully.

"How?"

"How do I ta...ta...talk?" The Monkey scorned again. "Magic."

Horatio stood silent watching this creepy creature talk and dance happily.

"Where did you come from?"

"Come closer and I'll show you," the monkey motioned with one long furry finger.

Instead of moving forward Horatio stepped back away from the monkey. As he stepped back he saw two shadows emerge from the other end of the alley. He squinted thinking that might help his vision, it usually did, but in this case he couldn't make out the shadows any clearer. One thing he was certain of was that whatever was causing those shadows were undoubtedly responsible for the child killings. Something shiny flashed in his vision.

"A blade?"

Was that a hatchet blade, Horatio thought. There was a most horrible feeling racing through his chubby body. The horrible feeling that filled him reminded Fat Kid of the same depressing chill he received from the now destroyed Winkie House.

"Magic?" Horatio said stepping further away from the dancing monkey.

He didn't take his eyes off the magical creature until he reached the front of the Impossible Dreams Thrift Store. The lights were still on.

"Thank god," Fat Kid said not realizing that he had in fact taken his eyes off the monkey. And when he looked back - "Gone?"

Horatio stared at the exact spot where he had just seen the dancing monkey, but it was missing. Had he actually seen that monkey? He only had to walk ahead to realize that the monkey was real. Horatio glanced at the poop on the bottom of his sneaker.

"It was real," he said not knowing if this made him happier or more frightened.

#

The lights were on but no one seemed to be home at the Impossible Dreams Thrift Store. Fat Kid shielded his eyes against the street lamp's reflection on the front window's grimy glass. He saw the aisles of thrift store junk and the front counter where Tom usually stood, but the place was empty.

Checking his wristwatch he noticed that fifteen minutes had passed since he set out from his place. Horatio looked down the street from which he had come and noticed the flashing neon dragon sign for The Golden Dawn Chinese Restaurant. He still had some pocket money from the allowance his father gave him before he left. Sweet and Sour chicken and noodles sounded just about right at that moment.

So Horatio headed back down the street to the Chinese restaurant.

The crisp autumn leaves rustled along the sides of the buildings on Cobb Street. The curfew wouldn't take effect for another hour. That would give him time to have some dinner and then race back home. Heck, he might even find the time to finish his math homework. Fat Kid smiled at that as he pulled open the door to the restaurant.

"Wow," Horatio whispered.

It was warm in there. He saw the steam coming from the kitchen in the back of the place. The small lobby with its red tiles and oversized fish tank always made him feel welcome and cozy. The exotic fish that swam lazily in the clear water of their tank were always fascinating to him. They were so large that sometimes Fat Kid had the feeling that they were watching him the way a shark might if he was in the deep blue sea. He had no doubt that under the right circumstances those exotic fish might just take a nibble from him. Fat Kid looked at his chubby fingers.

"You certainly have enough meat," he whispered to himself.

"Hello, just one?"

A pleasant voice came to him from his left and Fat Kid turned once seeing a pretty Oriental hostess standing in front of him.

"Ah, yes please. Just me," he said.

"Follow me," the hostess led Horatio into the dining area which was quite large despite the outside of the place, which looked like a small hole in the wall storefront take-out joint.

"Thanks."

Fat Kid followed her to a small booth and after the hostess took his drink order he excused himself. His bladder felt like it was suddenly going to spill over. It was also Horatio's custom to wash his hands before a meal.

"Down stairs to right…keep right. You not go left. Left *very* bad. Keep right," the hostess said and as she spoke she became more and more aggravated.

"Right, I'll stay to the right. Got it," Horatio said as he walked the length of the dining area and then found a small alcove that led to a steep flight of stairs. "Keep right."

Fat Kid reached the bottom. The place was dark and creepy. Two single bulbs attached to a wall sconce were used to light the entire area. He looked right first and barely made out the His and Hers restrooms. Looking left he saw nothing but darkness. The interior of this basement felt cavernous and strange. He turned toward the right when he heard something bellow in the darkness to his left, something that did not sound human. Horatio sprinted to the restroom and slammed the door before he realized that he was standing in the pitch black.

That bellow came again but softer now that he was inside the restroom.

Horatio extended his arms because he had no idea where the light switch was. Slowly he tip-toed forward and…

"Ouch!"

He bumped his forehead on something solid. That hurt, he thought but then felt the item in front of him. It was metal, a stall maybe? He couldn't believe how turned around he got just being in here for a matter of seconds.

"So if that's the stall in front of me that means the door should be around…"

Horatio reached around and felt the door frame.

"The light switches are usually…Bingo," he said flicking the switch that he felt against the wall.

When the lights burst on he almost screamed. Someone was standing right in front of him. Fat Kid took a step back covering his face with his plump hands. As he peered through his fingers he noticed that he was looking at his own reflection in the grime splattered mirror.

"Ha, scared of your own shadow Horatio," he whispered, chuckling at the comedy of it.

After tending to his business he washed his hands, only to find out that there were no paper towels and the hand dryer was broken.

"Great," he moaned wiping his hands on the seat of his jeans as he turned to leave.

But as he approached the door he stopped and listened. That creepy bellowing did not come and so after several more tentative seconds he exited the restroom and sprinted for the stairs that would lead him back to the cozy dining room.

When he reached the bottom of the steep stairs he heard a howling this time and Charlie Bokar's face appeared in his mind. It must have been Charlie Bokar dressed in his werewolf mask trying to scare him. Yeah that made sense.

"Nice try Charlie, but I…" This time when the bellow came he felt the goose flesh on his plump body run cold and the hair stood on end as he raced up the stairs as fast as he could.

When he reached the top of the stairs he was sweating like a pig, huffing and puffing. As he walked down the center aisle of the dining room he noticed diners eating and laughing. When he went back to his booth the hostess was standing there staring at him. Fat Kid wiped a layer of sweat off his forehead and coughed, about to slide into the booth.

"No sit down. You went left. I tell you go right!" The hostess was shouting at him now.

His face went red and he lowered his head in his usual submissive pose as the hostess yelled in Chinese at him and then shooed him from the restaurant. Eyes watched him from the other patrons. His red face went scarlet as he was tossed out the front door.

"Crap," Horatio said as he looked back at the hostess who was still yelling in Chinese at him through the front window.

Chapter Three

Buried in piles of books so dusty no vacuum cleaner or sweeper could ever get them fully clean, sat Tom chewing on his soggy cigar. He was in the bowels of the Impossible Dreams Thrift Store. Many archaic books on mythology, demonology and a dozen other studies lay open in front of him on an old Formica table. A hanging green-shaded lamp illuminated the scene.

Tom wore a pair of glasses and looked quite scholarly as he scanned through a spirit guide book that focused on demon possession. He had seen this brutality before. The Hatchet of Borden was not the proper name for the evil inside the relic but Lizzie Borden was the most famous killer who used it. Many researchers believed that the weapon she used was a simple farmer's ax, but further paranormal investigation proved that the blade used on her father's head was that of a hatchet.

Tom removed his glasses and wiped his tear ridden eyes with an old cloth handkerchief.

"Demons," he groaned. "Ah, who needs'em."

Tom blew out a smog of smoke from his cigar and then slid his glasses back on and he fingered the current text in front of him which was Tobin's

Spirit Guide. He was currently reading a cliff notes version on Doppelgangers. These were nasty demons who took the image of a person they possessed and could do all kinds of mischief, like *murder*. Tom suspected that the hatchet killer fell into this category because of the last users of the hatchet. He would need more time to pick through these old tomes to be sure. If his theory about who wielded the hatchet was correct they were all in major trouble.

The idea of the Doppelgangers made him wince. Tom wasn't one to drudge up the past when it pertained to him and his kind. The past was the past.

"Dead and buried," he said to himself.

Looking around the dark basement he wondered how many entities locked away down here were watching and waiting for him to make a mistake again. Nothing lasted forever. Each entity caged in their prison would find a way out. The war was never done. Battling evil-doers was a full time job throughout eternity and Tom was locked into it for the long haul.

"Doppelgangers," he whispered again as he removed an old washed out picture.

The picture contained two young girls maybe thirteen years old. They were smiling, dressed in summer dresses while standing in the sunlight.

"Oh my sweethearts…" Tom said whistling an old blues tune under his breath as he looked lovingly at the twins in the picture.

When the maddening howl came from the darkness surrounding him Tom jumped. The pain and anger in that sound was so horrible and unexpected that Tom pulled his lighter and flicked the wick.

"Who's there?" He called out into the dark. His eyes were already watering with tears from his own memories. These tears made it even more difficult for the old rogue to see.

When the howl did not return he killed the lighter and closed up a couple of the more choice tomes and started for the rickety stairs. As he reached the steps Tom stared up and saw two young girls silhouetted at the top of the stairs. Tom's old heart took another leap into his throat as he saw them staring down at him. Because they were silhouetted he couldn't make out the true features of their faces. What he did see clearly was what they held.

"The Borden Hatchet," Tom said.

"No, not Borden. Much older than Borden. Much older than Tom."

The girls, if they were girls, and Tom definitely felt like whatever stood at the top of his stairs wasn't human at all, spoke in unison and then giggles.

"Tell me demons, if you are demons, what are your names?"

The silhouettes just shook their heads and raised the hatchet. Suddenly the books Tom carried burst into flames.

"Oh, gosh!"

Tom dropped the books onto the concrete floor of the basement and tried desperately to stamp them out, but the more he stamped the higher the flames grew. The books on the table under the green-shaded lamp also burst into flames.

"Oh crap," Tom said as he ran to the table knocking it over.

As the burning books hit the floor they became nothing but burnt embers. Tom approached the ash toeing the remains. He noticed how the remains were now nothing but a filthy patch of smudge.

Tom turned back toward the stairs when he saw a small colorfully dressed monkey standing on its head along the top of the stairs.

"Monkey?"

"Old ugly human," the monkey screeched sticking out its purple tongue and then it threw something at Tom.

Whatever it was slapped him in the face. Tom wiped it off his scruffy chin only to realize that it was monkey feces.

"Why you little..." Tom sprinted up the stairs but the monkey was quicker. He slammed the door on old Tom sealing him off in the dark basement.

#

Somewhere else in the city as evening pressed on to full night children cried in their beds. Parents held their loved ones and whispered sweet promises of sunlight and fun. Deep in the belly of the DenMark city lurked the fracture in the proverbial egg keeping the creepy crawlies from the citizens' doorsteps. Evil slipped through and bigger evils chipped slowly away at this fracture awaiting their time to enter the physical world.

Across the city in their little dingy flat Nick and Fish stayed up watching an all-night horror festival from a station out of Pittsburg.

Fish was lounging on the couch under an afghan his mother made him. Nick was in the kitchen cooking dinner. It was after eight-thirty in the p.m. but the boys liked to eat late. The call came across Fish's cell phone. He moaned and groaned when he heard the buzzer.

"Fish, bud, get up. Cell's ringing," Nick called from the kitchen.

"I hear it," Fish grumbled back.

He was too cozy to be bothered with another call. Besides. these October nights in DenMark were bloody cold.

The cell continued to buzz.

"Fish!" Nick shouted.

"Got it," he called back.

He snagged the buzzing cell and answered the call.

"Ya got the Fish – speak."

"Hello, is this the paranormal investigators?"

Fish heard the voice of an old granny talking into his waxy ear.

"That we be. Who be you?"

"Who I am isn't important. What I have to tell you is. Somewhere in the bowels of this city is something evil…"

"No kidding sister. This is DenMark. Be more specific," Fish said.

The voice changed from a sweet sounding old lady to a terrible thunderstorm trapped in a human vessel.

"*THE WORLD IS COMING TO AN END AND YOU WILL ALL DIE!*"

Fish pulled the cell away from his ear. He could practically feel the ectoplasm of this thing crawling through the cell phone.

"Yuck, lady I appreciate the head's up but I've known the human race is being flushed for years. Now I asked for specifics. Give up or shut up," Fish said.

He had switched the cell phone to speaker mode. Nick, with his tie loosened and cuffs rolled up wearing a stained apron, entered the living room. He had overheard the caller's voice.

"THE BASEMENT OF THE CITY. CRACKS HAVE OPENED AND THE EVIL HAS LEAKED THROUGH. MUST CLOSE THESE CRACKS."

"Got an address?"

"226 COBB STREET."

The line went dead.

"226 Cobb Street? That's pretty specific," Nick said.

"226 Cobb Street, heck dude, that's The Golden Dawn Chinese restaurant."

"You sure?"

Fish pulled out his hack license and flashed it at Nick.

"I drive a taxi don't I? 'Course I know every address in this frickin city. Let's suit up," Fish said pushing back his afghan.

Suiting up for these would-be ghost hunters meant slipping into their gray and brown corduroy coveralls with the homemade Ghost Hunters patches on the front pockets. Nick had them designed by a local artist named Jim Weed. Nick also had van magnets made up with that same logo.

Their VW van was already loaded with all of their ghost and demon hunting equipment. Nick was great with that. Fish wasn't so together when it came to being prepared for stuff. But his buddy always had things covered. Besides being organized, Nick was a wizard in techno magic junk. It was his bread and butter. Literally. Nick made a living offering an online store for his ghost and demon catching inventions. They sold like crazy. He currently held a patent on a dozen of these devices, as well as having a number of other patents pending.

"Here," Nick threw Fish the keys.

Fish always drove. Nick pretty much did everything else.

"Okay Flo, we got a live one. Let's roll," Fish said sliding the key into the VW ignition. He always tried to coax the old van into starting by using her name. Flo had a flooding problem that always annoyed Nick, so Fish tried to be smooth with their van like it was an actual gal.

"Flo? Jeez Fish. You know one of these days those old VHS tapes of ALICE are going die a horrible death," Nick said.

"Watch your mouth. ALICE was the best show ever on the boob tube – Flo! With a wife like Florence Jean Castleberry I wouldn't need to bunk with you," Fish said lighting a cigarette as Flo, the VW van, sped off into the night shooting out a cloud of exhaust.

#

Flo arrived at 226 Cobb Street a couple of minutes later with Nick and Fish inside. They exited the VW van and grabbed their supplies from the back.

"What kinda entity do you figure we got here?" Fish asked as he flicked his cigarette into the alley trash.

"Not sure, but I do happen to know that a little girl, Margie Miles, was murdered here five nights ago. Horrible case. Apparently, without being too graphic, she was hacked up with a hatchet," Nick said, as Fish smirked.

"Not too graphic, eh Nicky-boy?"

Nick shrugged strapping on his back pack. Inside that pack were five inventions that he always carried. These pretty much covered all the entities that he knew of that existed within the DenMark borders.

"Hacked up a poor kid with a hatchet? Doesn't sound supernatural to me."

"No but that voice on the cell sure was, and since it sent us to the very location that the murder happened, well, I'd say we're dealing with a level seven entity," Nick said adjusting his shoulder straps.

"Remind me what a level seven is again."

"It's an entity that…" – Fish heard an encyclopedia definition coming but cut Nick off before he could get too far into it.

"Cliff notes dude," Fish said.

"Right, well they can pretty much mess with a human both physically and psychologically."

"No kidding? Maybe we oughta go through which tools might work best on a level seven ghoul," Fish suggested.

"*Entity*, actually. Ghouls rob graves."

Nick saw Fish's irritated expression and pushed ahead.

"Okay," he said unzipping Fish's pack.

Nick pulled out a small black square box with a red RadioShack logo on it. Attached to the box was a 1980's style headset – big, bulky, and unhip. The buttons along the front of the box were different colors; red, blue, and green.

"We've gone through this before but just as a recap, and we'll do the cliff notes version. Okay, three buttons – red, blue, and green. Red stops the device. The green activates it…"

"And the blue?"

"Don't ever touch the blue button. Here," Nick said as he hit a small black switch on the edge of the box.

Fish immediately smelled the stink of burnt ozone.

"You sure that thing is safe? Stinks like it's got a short in it."

"Trust me this is grade-A equipment," Nick assured him with a smile.

"You know my uncle used to say RadioShack products are junk."

"What's he do again?"

"Garbage man," Fish said.

"Case made. Put the headphones on. Once the device is activated we will have an audio link which will isolate everything outside of the headphones so we can only hear each other. That eliminates audio entity intrusion."

"Cool," Fish said as he took the box and noticed how it had a belt clip on the back. He clipped it to his coveralls pocket and slid the headphones on.

Nick did the same with his own device. Nick pressed the green button and motioned for Fish to follow suit. Fish pressed the button and heard Nick's voice immediately. Everything else in the city went silent.

"Amazing," Fish said.

"Thanks, kinda of proud of this invention myself. So the basic idea is this device keeps our minds safe, locked away from any outside forces. Since we're just doing a reconnaissance mission tonight I didn't bring the big guns. What I did bring, and you have one in your pack too, is The Hose."

"*The Hose*? Cool I like The Hose. What's The Hose?" Fish asked.

"Man you never listen when I explain a new invention. We used The Hose last week on a level three entity on Bleaker Street," Nick said.

"Don't lecture me dude just show me how it works."

Nick just shook his head and lifted what looked like a mini-vac with some serious modifications. The device's hose was a standard vacuum cleaner hose about six feet long. It was attached to a small sack that looked like a canvas bag. The bag fit over shoulder with a strap.

"The Hose sucks in most entities, even level seven. Theoretically of course," Nick said blushing.

"Theoretically?"

"Well, yeah. I mean it's not like we've encountered a level seven entity yet."

Nick just shrugged.

"Whatever dude. Let's do this. I wanta watch Letterman in half an hour," Fish said checking his Mickey Mouse wristwatch.

Nick pulled out a third item. This was simply a standard remote tracker that had been set up to follow frequency waves for a level seven entity. A small dial on the top of the device had multiple settings depending on which level entity that you wanted to track. The dial went up to eight levels.

"Okay I think we're ready," Nick said shouldering his Hose and making sure everything on his utility belt was operational.

"Lead the way Kemosabe."

Fish lit another cigarette and followed his friend into the dark alley that would bring them out onto 226 Cobb Street.

Fish took note that even for eleven o'clock at night the shadows filling this alley looked darker somehow, like maybe someone had painted the walls with a flat black ink. He couldn't make out any characteristics of the alley walls or street at all. He didn't even see the dumpster until he bumped into it, and that's when he noticed that he couldn't see Nick either in front of him and the fear really started to take hold then.

"Bro, where are you?"

When he didn't hear any reply from Nick, Fish tossed aside his cigarette and pressed the green button to activate the black device that he had attached to his waist, making sure it was still on. He heard nothing except his own voice. The sound of his own voice in a vacuum frightened him and he reached out to try and touch Nick.

"Nick dude, don't play around man. I can't see you bro," Fish said hearing the fear in his voice.

Fish lifted the hose to his weapon and flicked the ON switch.

"Okay entities, I'm ready for you."

When something bumped into him he grabbed it and almost swung.

"Fish?"

"Nick? Dude where the heck were you man? You scared the crap out of me," Fish said.

He still was unable to see his partner but he held Nick's shoulder in his right hand.

"Nick I think maybe we oughta back outta here and regroup. What do ya say?"

"I SAY IT'S TIME TO DIE!"

This was the same creepy voice that Fish had heard over the cell phone back at their flat. Immediately he switched on The Hose and the blackness began to subside. It was like a vacuum cleaner sucking up smoke. Within minutes the air in the alley was clearing and he saw Nick standing at the end of the alley about to step onto the street in front of The Golden Dawn Chinese restaurant.

"Nick!" Fish shouted as he ran to meet his friend.

Nick just looked at Fish like he had a screw loose.

"What's the matter?"

"Didn't you see it man? Or hear it?"

"See what? Hear what?"

"The blackness in the alley…the voice over the headphones. It was the same voice as on the cell dude," Fish said.

That's when Fish noticed how Nick was staring at him.

"What?"

"Your coveralls," Nick said pointing at Fish's gray corduroy coveralls. They were dripping with a black substance.

"Yuck, what is this stuff?"

"Ectoplasm residue," Nick said.

"Ecto-disgusting is what it is, yuck!"

"What happened to you?"

"I was like following you into the alley when this darkness surrounded me. It was so subtle I didn't notice it at first but, it couldn't have been more than a few seconds after stepping into the alley…crap, the voice," Fish said.

"The voice? You mean the one from the cell?"

"Yeah it said something about getting ready to die. We were gonna die dude," Fish said.

It wasn't often that Nick saw his friend scared or even agitated but Fish was both now.

"Calm down. We're safe. See?"

Nick motioned to the well-lit street in front of the Chinese restaurant. A few cars drove past looking at the weird guys in their jumpsuits and strange equipment.

Fish threw a gob of the black ectoplasm onto the street and was amazed to see it started to crawl away. Nick also watched this in amazement. He quickly sucked up the ectoplasm with his hose. A second later he and Fish were running the hose up and down Fish's coveralls sucking the black substance into the canvas bag. When Fish was as clean as they could get him Nick pressed a white button that Fish hadn't noticed was attached to the sack.

"Ah Fish, I think we better get the heck out of here," Nick said.

"Why?"

"Because The Hose's scale tells me that this ectoplasm is from a very powerful entity," Nick said.

"What level?"

"Off the charts man."

They both turned back toward the alley which was nothing but a wall of black smoke now. A second later they heard a grinding laughter inside the smoke and they bolted down the street as far away from that smoke as they could get.

Chapter Four

It was almost midnight by her cat-faced clock. The clock hung off the wall in her bedroom. The tail ticked the time by swaying back and forth like a metronome. Rachel loved to watch that mechanical tail move left and right, left and right. Tonight though, she was too distracted. It was technically a school night being Wednesday, or Thursday morning depending on your choice. Being a school night she normally went to bed early, but her mother was still out and she was starting to get scared.

Her only solace was her vampire gown that she had palmed from the old wooden foot locker at The Impossible Dreams almost a year ago. The others were distracted with some talk about horse racing and Rachel moseyed back to where Tom had kept the footlocker stored. She wasn't proud of the theft, but unlike Horatio and the Bokar Brothers, she had nothing else to depend on. Horatio had his parents who loved and supported him, and even though Charlie and Henry Bokar didn't really have parents, they had each other.

Rachel was simply alone.

She removed the gown from her bottom dresser drawer and held it up looking at her reflection in the cracked oval mirror above the dresser. She had to admit that she was becoming quite a looker. Her body, now twelve, had taken on a shape and form of a woman. Of course her current girl's shapes were nothing like the ones she had while in the vampire gown. She smiled thinking about the gown and the powerful change that it caused in her.

The books on her dresser, the ones with the golden five-pointed stars also made her feel powerful.

"Rachel?"

She heard her mother's voice calling to her from the other side of her bedroom door. When had her mother gotten home?

"Mom, leave me alone. I'm trying to sleep," Rachel called back.

"Honey, open up *please*?"

Was that urgency in her mother's voice? Rachel hadn't heard that tone for quite some time. She lowered the gown but carried it to the door.

"Mom, is everything okay?"

She stepped closer to the door when a massive blow struck the cheap wood. The material started to split immediately. Rachel fell back against her bed. The second hit broke the door open as a hulking man stepped through the scraps of wood dangling from the frame. He was drunk and ugly as a troll.

"Hey little one. How you doin'." The guy's drunken slobber disgusted Rachel.

She knew the man, he was one of her mother's regular beaus, Ted...something, and he was a mean drunk.

"Ted, leave her alone!" Ilene Brooks screamed at the thug.

He just looked back at her grinning like an idiot. He scanned the small bedroom noticing what a mess it was when his eyes lit on a pile of books on her desk. Along the spine of the books there were archaic titles like The Necronomicon, and Grimoires with five-pointed stars in gold leaf.

"Witch!" Ted shouted. He pointed drunkenly at the books on Rachel's desk. "Look there. Yer brat's a witch!"

"Ted, stop it," Ilene Brooks was in tears now.

Rachel was still on the ground but she felt an internal rage strike her. She had cowered away from her mother's goons for too long. Tonight it ended.

She got to her feet and screamed into Ted's sweaty drunken face.

"Get out of my room. Get out of our trailer and…"

Ted cracked her across the lips with one heavy massive paw. Rachel fell back onto the bed tasting warm blood. Ilene screamed. Instead of cowering away like she had for so many nights she glanced down at the gown and smiled. Ilene was pulling at Ted's large arm and he turned to face her.

"Ya tramp. Don't you ever touch me," he shouted and slapped Ilene across the face.

Ilene fell back striking her head on the hallway floor. Her eyes rolled for a second and she was out cold. When he turned back to Rachel she had been replaced by a…

"A vampire? Halloween ain't for a couple of weeks sweet cheeks," Ted said laughing at his amateurish poetics.

Rachel was fully garbed in her vampire gown, stolen from The Impossible Dreams footlocker. The magic that flowed in her now was wonderful. It raced along every cell in her body and she felt her stature grow. When Ted noticed how she increased in size his eyes did the same.

"Waa..waa…" Ted mumbled as he saw her levitate before his eyes.

"No not a witch," she hissed and snatched him around the scruffy throat. "I would rip out your filthy throat if you didn't stink so much."

She lifted him off his feet carrying him down the hallway and out the front door. When they were outside she flew with Ted into the air, high above the trees. They could see the city skyline from here with all of its grimy light twinkling like devil's eyes beneath them.

Rachel closed her eyes and smelled the night, relishing in the darkness of it.

When she opened her eyes she had almost forgotten that she was still holding Ted. If she released him now he would be crushed by the fall, they were miles up. Rachel took pleasure when she noticed that he had peed himself.

"You will never return to my mother's trailer. If I ever see you again I'll drop you. Understand?"

Ted shook his head frantically.

"Yes…yes! I promise! I'll never so much as look yer mother's way! Let me go! Let me go," he screamed.

"Are you sure you want me to let you go?"

"*Set me DOWN! Set me down!*"

Rachel glared at him once more and her eyes glistened in the moonlight. She felt the urge to just drop him. She felt it grow so strongly in her that she could almost not stop it. This must be how Horatio felt when he saved them from Winkie Witch - the total corruption of power. Over the last year they had barely talked, she and Horatio, but he had warned her that he had an inner demon that seemed to want him to always wear the suit, like a junky needing a fix. It scared him. It scared her now too.

She quickly dropped to within ten feet of Ted's pick-up truck and then she dropped him into the bed. He scrambled out drunkenly over the side and slid behind the wheel where he started it and floored it out of the Industrial Trailer Park. Gravel flew in the air as the pickup sped off into the night. Rachel watched for miles as Ted swerved on the unlit roads of DenMark. The night was beautiful. She meant to explore it now that her mother was safe and the gown had fully embraced her.

#

They found themselves at Ralph's, an all-night pizza joint on Branch Street. Fish and Nick were still in their ghost hunter corduroy coveralls. Flo, their VW van, was parked out front within eye sight. Ralph's Pizzeria wasn't a usual hang out for the roomies but tonight they needed coffee. Nick was guzzling the black tar and Fish was chain smoking.

"Dude I think this ghost hunting stuff's for the birds. You're right about catching level one or two ghosts, but man what I experienced in that alley with all that black smoke was like nothing I *ever* want to experience again," Fish said dragging on cigarette.

"Yeah, I have to admit that entity was more than we're ready to handle, but maybe Tom has something that can help," Nick said thoughtfully.

"Old Tom? You kidding. That guy's wacked. Dude if you want to go back to that alley then that's all you man, all *you*."

Fish snuffed his cigarette and downed his coffee.

"So you're just going to abandon this city to whatever evil is lurking in that alley?"

"Dude, I got a good gig," Fish said removing his hack license from the front pocket of his coveralls. "This ghost hunting thing's always been yer thing more than mine."

Nick looked long and hard at his friend and then felt the tears of abandonment burn his eyes. Nick had always had a thing about abandonment. He was an orphan and had almost no ties to anyone outside of Fish. Fish had teased him in the past about moving out but Nick never actually thought his friend would follow through with it.

"Gotta go. Shift starts in about an hour, gotta get cleaned up first," Fish said sliding from the booth.

Nick wiped at his eyes as he sat there pouting.

"Dude look, I'm not goin' anywhere anytime soon. But, geez we're talkin' what? Demons?"

"Technically it's more of an energy…"

Fish held up one grubby hand for his friend to stop talking.

"Cliff notes version."

"It's an energy source, where it comes from and what's powering it, we don't know. But once we find out we can stop it," Nick said.

"Like flicking a switch?"

"Like flicking a switch."

Nick seemed satisfied with that analogy.

"Let's get home and clean up. Then you can start doing research on whatever the heck this black cloud can be."

Nick dropped some bills on the table as they headed for the door.

"Adios muchachos," Ralph called from the kitchen.

The boys nodded and left.

#

Here he was again. Another night over the hump. It was Thursday now. His dad was still gone. His mother was out for the first time in weeks. She went to her sister's across the neighborhood. Horatio was alone. Nothing on the television. Nothing he wanted to eat in the kitchen and the street lights were on outside. Fat Kid looked at his gut sticking out over his jeans and then he switched off the TV and went to the hallway closet where he removed his jacket and sneakers and left the house.

Horatio walked down Elm Street to Gotham and then skipped Bradbury by entering the alley that would take him to Cobb Street. The police tape was gone now. It was a school night but like his mom showed him – who cared. The only thing that concerned him was what he had seen the previous night. Roscoe the monkey and those two shadows. Before entering Horatio looked into the alley. It seemed okay. The shadows were there but they matched the objects casting them. There wasn't so much as a single creepy feeling now. Looking once more over his shoulder at the normalcy of Gotham Street on a week night Horatio entered the alley.

He was halfway down the space when he saw a young guy, mid-twenties, kneeling in the opening at the other end of the alley. Horatio stopped walking and stared at the guy. The guy stared back. He was holding some strange device with the words RadioShack on it.

"What are you doing kid? Are you crazy? Get out of there now!"

The fear in the guy's voice startled Horatio. He looked back the way he had come and sure enough there was a dark swarm beginning to form. It was coming from the walls and the floor of the alley.

"Come on kid move it!"

Horatio sprinted forward. The darkness behind him was collecting in mid-air. Horatio watched over his shoulder and then stumbled face first into a pile of garbage cans. He felt the cutting of his cheek against something sharp in one of the trash bags and winced. The tears came next followed by terror that not even Winkie Witch had caused.

The guy looked at whatever the darkness was becoming and Horatio saw the guy's eyes go wild. To Horatio's surprise despite the guy's horrible expression he was racing forward into the alley to grab him.

"Don't look back kid trust me don't..."

"What is it?"

Horatio was full-on crying now, tears drenching his plump cheeks. The stranger had him by the wrists and he yanked with all of his might. The guy must have barely weighed as much as Fat Kid, who was only eleven. As they tumbled out onto the street Horatio fell on the guy. They were both covered in sweat and something else, something black and gooey.

"Back up," the guy shouted.

Fat Kid was on his stomach and then rolled to his back and saw the darkness as it formed a giant face and snarled at them. The guy next to him was holding something up in the air over Horatio's head. The face shifted and its empty eyes stared from Fat Kid to the guy with the, whatever it was that he held in his hands.

"HAHAAAAA!" The giant face bellowed at the man, but when the guy flicked a switch on his hip the thing's face lost its amused expression replaced by another scowl.

The black device the guy was holding was obviously some sort of tool because when the switch was flicked Horatio heard something that sounded like a vacuum cleaner. Some of the dark stuff in the air was quickly absorbed into the canvas bag that was attached to the tool. The bag increased in size and the guy was reading what looked like some kind of a monitor.

"What is that?"

"Shhh!"

The guy switched off the vacuum tool and smiled at the monitor.

"Come on kid let's get out of here," the guy said. As they turned to leave they heard a voice.

"Be seeing you," the voice slithered.

Horatio and his new friend looked at the speaker and saw the small monkey, Roscoe.

"That's it. That's the monkey I saw before - the one that talks. You heard it right?"

"Yeah," the guy said as he lifted his tool again but the monkey shrieked at them and ran off into the shadows of the alley.

"Tell me you saw all of that," Horatio said.

"All of it. My name's Nick, what's yours?"

"Horatio, but everyone just calls me Fat Kid."

"Come on kid, you hungry?"

"Does a bear poop in the woods," Fat Kid asked feeling humor start flooding back into him.

"I guess it does," Nick said. "Come on."

Nick motioned to the VW van.

"Cool. That yours?"

"Yeah this is Flo. Flo this is Horatio."

"Fat Kid, please," Horatio corrected him.

"FK?"

Horatio thought about the initials and smiled.

"Yeah, FK. I like it."

They slid into Flo and the VW van sputtered off into the night.

#

"Fish, man look at this reading," Nick said.

He had just slammed on Flo's brakes and exited the VW van after he pulled into a parking lot next to the Graham's Town Hall Theater. The parking lot was a hot spot for cabbies in downtown DenMark because on any night of the week the Town Hall was open as a twenty-four hour theater playing films of all eras and genres.

"Dude calm down, bring it in here," Fish said dragging on his cigarette as he motioned his fellow cabbies off. There was a small group of taxi drivers watching this little scene with some humorous interest.

"Fish, check these readings man. Now I'm completely convinced that we're dealing with a combination entity..."

"Nick bro, quiet down dude."

Fish was watching as his fellow cabbies were glaring at Nick and the strange fat kid in the front seat of the VW van. Fish took Nick around the shoulders and led him back to the van. When he saw Fat Kid in the van he looked back at Nick.

"What's with the fat kid, man?"

"Oh, that's Horatio, F.K., he was present at the last attack."

"Last attack, dude did you go back to that alley?"

"Well first I went back to our flat and did some research, but man, based off these new readings I'd say we're dealing with a Fright, a Spiritus, or maybe even a Doppelganger. I mean if what the paper is saying is correct..."

"Nick stop!"

"What, man?"

Fish opened the driver side door of the van and motioned for his friend to get in.

"Go home. Take that kid to his place and put your feet up. Relax. I'll bring some take-out home later. Just promise me to stay away from that alley," Fish said.

"Fish, buddy, you're not listening to me man. I have readings here that if properly analyzed we

72

might be able to breakdown the compounds that make up this entity. Its science man, just science," Nick said excited.

Fish saw the remnants of black ectoplasm on Nick's corduroy coveralls.

"Get those covers cleaned and go home man," Fish said.

He was done talking as he turned away and headed back to his group of cabbies.

"Fish..."

"Go home," Fish shouted back.

Nick sat in silence for a minute and then looked at Horatio who was gobbling down a hero sandwich that Nick had bought him at Ralph's Pizzeria earlier.

"Thanks for the sandwich," Fat Kid said between large bites.

"Sure," Nick said.

He was clearly thinking, and trying to figure out their next move.

"I don't know if this would help but I know a guy who knows a lot about this kinda stuff. You know, magic and junk. Maybe we should stop by his place," Horatio said stuffing the rest of the sandwich in his mouth. Mustard and mayo was smeared across his lips and cheeks.

"Horatio I just don't know. Maybe Fish is right. Maybe we should call it a night," Nick said.

"Are you kidding me? That darkness in the alley has gotta be responsible for the death of those two kids. Now I don't know about you but if I went home and another kid died or went missing I couldn't live with myself."

Nick blew out all his stress and frustration as he looked through the bug stained windshield of Flo and saw Fish smoking and laughing with the other cabbies like he wasn't almost gobbled up by some black ectoplasm last night.

"Okay Horatio. Who's this friend of yours?"

#

"Tom, you here?" Charlie had just opened the front door to The Impossible Dreams. He and Henry had an extra set of keys made without Tom's knowing. It never hurt to plan ahead.

It was true that they did the occasional *Turn* for Tom but sometimes those didn't pay the rent. Some of the artifacts, the lesser magical ones, did. Charlie would pilfer something small from here or there and sell it on eBay to crazy cult collectors. It kept him and Henry off the streets.

"Coast is clear," Charlie said grinning like the Devil.

"Okay Chuck but listen, nothing major. Something small," Henry said but Charlie was already walking down one of the aisles sticking stuff in his pockets.

"Cool, look at this."

Charlie lifted a twisted mummified hand.

"The Hand of Glory. Bad news bro," Henry said. "Leave it."

"How much do you think some of this junk's worth?"

"Depends on the bidder," Henry said. "Wait? Do you hear something?"

Charlie stopped moving for a minute and looked at his brother. He was about to say something but Henry lifted his finger to silence him. Henry was right, there was definitely something coming from the door at the end of the aisle, the door that led down to...the *basement*. They had both worked for old Tom for a long time and neither of them *ever* went downstairs.

"If you think I'm going down in that spooky basement in this haunted place you're nuts," Charlie whispered.

"Come on," Henry said tip-toeing to the end of the aisle.

They stopped in front of the door and listened.

"Hank let's blow this joint. Old Tom told us about that place down below. He don't want us down there," Charlie whispered.

"Shhh!"

Henry was leaning forward placing his ear to the wooden surface of the door just as the door flew wide open.

"AHHHH!!"

The Bokar Brothers screamed at the same time. They hugged each other staring down at the figure that fell forward smoking on the worn out carpeting. They noticed the old Fedora first.

"Tom!" Henry raced to the old thrift store proprietor.

76

"Tom?" Charlie asked.

Tom was smoking all over. He was covered in black ectoplasm.

"Chuck? Hank?"

At first the Bokars thought it was Tom speaking but then they saw the two figures standing behind them by the front door.

"Horatio?"

"Tom...he's, ah," Henry said but couldn't finish as he pointed at Tom who was lying silent on the floor at their feet.

Fat Kid ran down the aisle like a major league baseball player stealing home base. When he reached them he stopped and stared down at Tom who was shaking all over. He was unconscious and his clothes were smoking, but Horatio couldn't see any flames on the old man. He dropped to the floor and patted Tom anyway.

A second later Nick was standing behind him. Henry and Charlie stared up at the new guy who was dressed in a brown corduroy jump suit with a strange utility belt strapped around his slim waist.

"Who's that?" Charlie asked as Fat Kid was turning Tom over.

"My name's Nick," Nick said as he pushed past them and looked down at Tom. "We need to get that stuff off him, or else…"

"Or else what?" Henry asked sounding both terrified and excited.

"You don't want to know."

Nick removed The Hose from his belt and switched it on. The black ectoplasm reacted immediately to the suck as Nick dropped to his knees and started to swallow several coats of the black goo with the long hose. The others just stood back and watched this guy acting like he was an Electrolux salesman displaying a new vacuum cleaner. Within minutes almost all the black goo was gone. There was still residue caught in the scruff of Tom's beard but when the old guy opened his watery eyes and looked at those standing around him he wiped the goo off his chin.

"Nicholas? Is that you?"

"Yeah Tom, it's me," Nick said helping Tom to his feet.

Fat Kid, Charlie and Henry all stared shocked that Nick knew old Tom.

"Well I'll be damned. You're looking good boy."

"Not a boy anymore Tom. Still fighting the good fight though thanks to you," Nick said blushing openly.

"Tom what the heck happened?"

Horatio was standing next to the old proprietor who stared at the Bokar Brothers and then back at Nick and then the old man started to cry.

"I gotta tell you fellas a tale and when it's through you might wanta throw me under the bus," Tom said.

They all stared at each other in awe.

Chapter Five

They were the love of my life, my babies, Melissa and Michelle. They were born, well, longer ago than you would probably believe. If I told you how old I was you'd lock me up. But to be honest it was before the telephone, television, and automobile. We lived then in a small two bedroom place further upstate in a small village on the edge of the Adirondack Region of New York State. I was never very social even back then, the girls were different. Whenever we visited town they always wore their prettiest dresses and attracted all kinds of, as far as I was concerned, unwanted attention.

It was just that kind of unwanted attention my girls attracted one autumn at dusk when they headed off to town. I was busy with my studies. Back then I was a scholar, believe or not, old Tom could theorize with the best of them. I was a searcher. Any kind of esoteric religion, philosophy, and just plain ritual was not beyond my trappings.

To be honest I think perhaps I was responsible for what happened to my little girls, and what's happening in this city today. A man once said if you look into the abyss too long the abyss will start looking into you. All of my studies in my youth were trying to open doors. In the 1960's we called that - 'The Doors of Perception.' It all meant the same thing. I was looking beyond. Experimenting with paths that others had barely walked down. Peeking through those same doorways rarely seen. But I believe that I opened just one too many of those metaphysical doors and that began the cracking, splintering of our reality. Over the years I've patch-worked as best as I can but the truth is the monsters are getting in.

My girls, oh lord, my babies fell victim to one of those horrible monsters.

There is a creature who is only known simply as The GERMAN. He targeted my girls, stole them away from me the way every nasty charlatan does. He comes from the darkest of worlds, a place called – The Keys To The Kingdom.

The searching for the child slayer can stop because I know who the killer is...

#

"You know who's killing the kids?" It was Horatio.

Tom nodded sadly.

"Well who is it?" Nick asked.

"The horrible, *demented*, Hatchet Sisters," Tom said blowing his nose and wiping his eyes with a filthy rag.

"Hatchet Sisters?" Charlie and Henry said.

Charlie sounded skeptical but Henry seemed fascinated.

"These Hatchet Sisters, you know them?" Nick asked.

They had moved into the front of the store. Tom and Nick were drinking coffee and the boys were just sitting on a variety of strange chairs that they had collected from the dusty corners of the shop.

Tom nodded, yes.

"Okay so then you know where we can find them?"

"More importantly where the *cops* can find them," Fat Kid said.

They all stared at Horatio like he was nuts. Even Nick gave him the cold shoulder.

"Coffin Kids take care of their own," Nick said.

"Coffin Kids?" Horatio asked.

"That's what Tom used to call us when Fish and I were boys," Nick said smiling nostalgically. "Isn't that right Tom?"

Tom removed a soggy cigar from behind his ear and lit it. He looked at Fat Kid and the Bokar Brothers.

"You fellas didn't think you was the first, did ya?"

He scratched his wooly gray hair beneath the brim of his sweaty Fedora. Charlie and Henry seemed stunned. Charlie was angry and Henry seemed heart broken. Tom just stared down red faced.

"So who are the Hatchet Sisters?" Fat Kid asked.

"My daughters," Tom whistled through tears and thick cigar smoke.

#

She was tucked away beneath the covers of her favorite blanket. The blanket with the butterflies and unicorns was nestled beneath her perfect pink chin. Her eyes stared at the open crack in the closet door. Even though she was under her favorite blanket and her mother told her nothing could hurt her while she was tucked in, the young girl was scared. Emily wanted to believe her mother and at first she did. When the monkey in the clown suit first appeared in her room, sneaking in from her dark closet, Emily was excited. The monkey was funny and it *talked*. Emily couldn't believe it at first, but on the third night when it came back and it said its name was Roscoe she blinked in belief.

Roscoe had told Emily about his friends and that his friends wanted to meet her. Emily wasn't sure she wanted to meet the friends of a talking monkey. After all, she was eight now and believing in talking monkeys, and friends of talking monkeys, seemed ridiculous. Roscoe said that his friends were two little girls, sisters, and they very much wanted to meet her. Emily refused but the monkey won her over by doing funny tricks and showing her magic. It was really amazing. She was tucked in her bed watching a magical talking monkey and her parents were in their bed down the hallway snoring away.

Finally Emily relented. Tonight was the night she would meet Roscoe's friends. She was excited and scared – a little nervous maybe too.

Emily yawned thinking they would never come but then the darkness in her closet started to change like it did every night when the monkey appeared. She felt her little heart beating so fast that it was

84

bound to leap from her chest. She kept one hand on her chest to keep her heart inside, and then giggled at how funny that idea was.

When she saw the monkey's paw emerge from the darkness she sat up. When the light came on overhead she cried out in fright.

"Ahhh!"

"Emily Anne Dixon? It's after midnight. Why are you still awake?"

Emily's eyes went from her mother back to the emerging monkey paw. It was gone. The darkness in her closet was gone too. Emily stared at this and started to cry.

#

Flying over the streets of DenMark was Rachel - the mistress of the night. After seeing her mother to bed the night before Rachel had stalked the city. She grinned her fangy grin thinking about how cheesy this tag line sounded. She may have been a full blown creature of the night but she still retained her cynical twelve-year-old personality. Her white gown flew around her like clouds in the wind. If she wasn't undead she might have frozen to death being up so high at such freezing temperatures. As it was Rachel loved the adrenaline she felt flying through the night air during the witching hour. This was her at her absolute best.

She would never give this gown back to Tom to be put in that horrible old footlocker. Never!

Her tongue licked the long pointed fang on the right side of her mouth and she tasted blood. Blood was beyond delicious. It was what allowed her to survive. She felt the coming wave of emotion and, *memories*? The last time that she had worn the suit she swore that she had attained memories of another. It was a bygone era before electricity was harnessed and the streets were lit not with electricity but with candle light. The city was smaller then. The dark forest surrounding DenMark was much more expansive and chock full of shadows. These shadows in turn were filled with creatures lurking, peering in from another world, tantalized with the knowledge that soon they would break the barrier into our world.

Rachel saw this over one hundred years ago. She saw this struggle between the light and dark. DenMark had always been ground zero for the gathering darkness at reality's door. Someone, a very long time ago helped open that door allowing in a flood of creatures. Some were beaten back; others remained, silently in the shadows. Rachel could feel now that the shadows surrounding the

DenMark streets were alive. It was a creature with thought and motive.

She glanced around and saw no shadows in the air where she flew. What could that mean? The city streets after midnight were drenched in inky blackness, and as Rachel watched aloft, those inky shadows took form and moved from house to house, apartment to apartment. Rachel was reminded of the stories about the angel of death that visited homes in the olden days. Hadn't she seen the olden days while in this gown? Hundreds of years, centuries gone past in her memory.

Now she watched large patches of inky darkness withdraw from a small house on Barker Street. A monkey, dressed all on bright silky color, led the darkness out from the house and down the block. The monkey was speaking to the darkness and the darkness spoke back.

"The child wasn't right. She wasn't the one. We'll find the one. Trust old Roscoe. He knows," the monkey said.

"We grow weary of you monkey. We want the one," the darkness was like an avalanche of voices, one tumbling over the other. They all sounded out of sorts. One voice sounded like a petulant child, while another sounded like the voice echoing down a deep well. All in all they were creepy.

Rachel flew as close as she could but stayed as far away from the gathering darkness as the monkey continued down the street. The gathering was so bizarre like one of those surreal paintings where the world tilts and your sense of order is ripped to shreds. At that moment Rachel made herself a promise. She would follow this monkey to his destination. Once there she would remember the spot and then find Horatio and the others. Whatever this monkey was, whatever that darkness was searching for, Rachel had no doubt that they would leave a path of death and destruction in their wake.

#

It was after midnight, which was not the most profitable time of night for a cabby, but it allowed Fish time to read and drink coffee. These were two of his favorite past times. He was doing that just then, parked in the lot next to Graham's Town Hall Theater when he saw the monkey dressed in the clown suit. Fish checked his mug of coffee smelling it for booze.

"All clear," he whispered as he watched the monkey walk down the street past the front of the Caprice.

It didn't seem to notice him, but he noticed it. He particularly noticed how the thing walked upright, like a man, not hunched over like a monkey. Seeing this thing walking casually but with some urgency kind of frightened him, especially after he started thinking about the growing darkness that he and Nick had witnessed in the alley by Cobb Street.

"This city's getting stranger and stranger," Fish said going back to his reading, when he heard the monkey start talking.

He dropped his paperback book on the floor next to him and sat up, rolling down his window to listen.

"The child wasn't right. She wasn't the one. We'll find the one. Trust old Roscoe. He knows," the monkey said.

"Holy cow, that monkey's not just speaking. It's speaking English," Fish whispered.

His first thought?

"Call Nick, Nick will know what to do."

He slid his cell phone from his pocket and speed dialed his roomie.

#

Nick was still reeling from Tom's full disclosure about the Hatchet Sisters being the killers and his daughters when his cell buzzed in his pocket. He checked his wristwatch and then the caller.

"Fish?"

Nick figured his roommate was calling to apologize for blowing him off earlier that night.

"Yeah, Nick here."

"Ah dude, where are you right now?"

"Impossible Dreams, why?"

"At the expense of sounding like I've tied one on. I'm watching a monkey in a clown suit walking and talking down the street. I think you need to see this," Fish said.

"A monkey in a clown suit?" Nick said.

Fat Kid perked up when he heard mention of the monkey.

"Ask him if it talks?" Horatio said.

"Yeah, Fish said it's walking and talking," Nick had the cell phone covered.

"Where's he at?" Tom asked.

"Fish, where are you? The usual spot?"

"You know it," Fish said.

"We'll be there shortly. Don't take your eye off the monkey in the clown suit," Nick said. He couldn't believe he just said that.

"I'm on him."

Fish killed the line.

"He's parked in Graham Town Hall Theater lot. We should be there in about ten minutes, come on."

Nick headed to the door followed by Charlie, Henry, and Fat Kid. When they reached the door they all looked back and noticed that Tom was still standing at the counter looking down not meeting their eyes.

"Tom what are you waiting for let's move it," Charlie said.

"No ah, I think its best I stay here. Maybe…ah," Tom continued to mumble.

They could all see the fear and shame on the old rogue's face. The Bokar Brothers looked at one another mystified. They had known Tom for quite some time and never saw him at a loss for words. Horatio saw the irritation in Nick's face and figured since he and Tom had a history there was a good reason for that expression. It still stung that Tom was being so beaten.

"Tom where's the footlocker?"

"Yeah good thinking Fat Kid," Charlie said. "I've been jonesing to put that werewolf mask back on." Charlie was scratching his rib cage like maybe he still had some fleas or mange from the last time he wore the mask.

"Tom? Where's the footlocker?"

Tom couldn't meet their eyes.

"Tom where is it?" Charlie sounded desperate now.

When Tom didn't answer Charlie ran to him and grabbed the front of his corduroy vest and shook the old man.

"Where is the footlocker you stupid old man?"

Tom's cigar fell from his lips and he let Charlie shake him until Henry and Horatio grabbed Charlie.

"Chuck stop!" Henry shouted.

"He's got it Hank. He's gotta have it," Charlie shouted back.

"Did someone steal it?" Fat Kid asked.

"We don't have time for this," Nick said.

He was at the door and through it.

"If the darkness in that alley next to Cobb Street is any indication of the power we are going to face *we need* that footlocker," Horatio said.

"Footlocker, eh? I seem to remember a footlocker in my day too."

Nick stepped back inside the shop and looked at Tom.

"That wasn't by chance the *same* footlocker was it Tom?"

Tom broke free of Charlie and looked at all of them for a moment.

"Nick you were special, like these fellas. You and Fish and my daughters. You were all part of my Coffin Kids," Tom said

"Coffin Kids sounds about right, because if we go back to Cobb Street without those costumes we might as well start nailing spikes into *our* coffins," Charlie said.

He was spitting mad now.

"Okay cut it out! Where are the costumes Tom?" Horatio asked.

"Remember when I showed you boys the missing Borden Hatchet? Well the footlocker was stolen around the same time. Once these murders started appearing I knew that they had returned. That *it* had returned."

"It, what?" Henry asked.

"*It* being the ultimate darkness. Horatio and me saw it tonight in the alley by Cobb Street where the first girl, Margie Miles, was murdered. It was like a black cloud of smoke formed out of the shadows. Fish saw it too. Fish, crap," Nick said and then sprinted for the door again.

#

Meanwhile Fish had exited his cab and was following the monkey down the street. It hadn't occurred to him before but the streets were unusually dead. He continued down the street trying to hide behind trash cans, street lamps, cars and anything else that that he could find. He wasn't sure why he was trying to hide since the monkey seemed occupied with speaking to itself, at least that's what Fish assumed it was doing since there wasn't another living soul on this street.

Speaking of living souls, where the heck with Nick?

Fish retrieved his cell phone from the front pocket of his brown corduroy slacks and dialed his friend. Nick picked up on the first ring.

"Dude, where the hell are you man?"

"I'm en route now. Flo was having some kickbacks. We should be approaching the lot in about five minutes," Nick said.

"Don't bother I'm about a block away still following the monkey."

"Be there in a sec," Nick said.

"Hey, don't hang up. Stay on the line. This monkey's kinda freaky you know."

"Fish I can't stay on the line."

"You can't stay on the line?"

"No," Nick said.

"Why?"

"Cops."

"Cops? You see any cops?"

"No, but my luck I keep talking to you on the cell and one will be lying in wait on one of these blocks," Nick said. "Oops gotta go, cops."

The line went dead and that's when Fish realized that he had taken his eyes off the monkey. He rounded the next block and then screamed at what he saw.

#

The police cruiser that was tailing the van passed them like a shark. Nick noticed the cop looking over at him briefly but then sped off around the block, which was where Nick and the boys were headed. As they reached the turn Nick slammed on the brakes. Fat Kid who was riding shotgun was buckled in but Charlie and Henry, sitting in the back, were not. The Bokar Brothers flew forward. Charlie started yelling about how incompetent Nick was as a driver but Henry stopped him as he pointed through the front windshield.

In front of them, extending about a mile into the air, was the black vapor-like dust that they had seen in the alley. It had expanded now. Nick saw Fish standing in front of it about to be devoured.

"Holy moly!" Henry said.

"It's gotten bigger," Fat Kid said.

"No foolin'," Charlie said. "Let's beat it man."

"That's Fish. We need to get Fish," Nick said pointing at the skinny guy, who looked a little like Shaggy from Scooby Doo.

"Hey Nimrod, get out of there!" Charlie was shouting out his side window now.

Fish didn't react and then the huge cloud of blackness targeted him shooting forward. They all watched as Fish's body jumped around like a Mexican jumping bean. It danced and swayed and if they weren't aware that he was being attacked they all might have laughed at what a horrible dancer he was.

The cop from the cruiser was now radioing in for backup. They all watched from inside the van but the cop was exiting the cruiser.

"No!" They all shouted at the cop.

He turned to see the van and the young people inside. Nick wasted no time now he exited Flo and ran around to her back cargo door. He snagged The Hose, but suspected that since this entity broke the mold regarding levels, The Hose wouldn't do much to stop it. Nick looked at the jostling Fish for a second longer and then he hit a side panel of the van. A small device popped out. This was a weapon of last resort because if it didn't work it could devastate the entire city.

"Better now than later," Nick whispered.

He grabbed the small device he called The Brainbuster and started cranking on the power lever. It was a self-contained power source, like one of the crank flashlights. That's where Nick got the idea. He wiped sweat from his forehead and slammed Flo's back hatch. Fish turned to face the others, eyes glowing green.

"Shoot, that stuff got him," Charlie shouted.

The cop pulled his sidearm and pointed it at Fish. The black ectoplasm had entirely vanished inside of Fish. As he approached the others he screamed. The echoes of that scream forced them all to cover their ears. The windows of the police cruiser exploded and the cop dropped his gun to cover his ears. Windows of the adjacent building imploded and the telephone and power cable wires split from their poles snaking about the street like giant black cobras.

"Get back inside Flo!" Nick shouted at Charlie and Henry who had exited the van. Horatio was still buckled into his seat staring in awe at the black cables as they snaked about the air. "Flo is grounded."

Henry dragged Charlie back to the van and pushed him inside. They slammed and locked the doors. Nick stepped forward. He was still wearing his ghost hunter coveralls and had his utility belt wrapped around his slim waist. In one hand he held The Hose and the other he had the Brainbuster.

The cop's eyes were fluttering and Nick noticed that whatever had hold of him was starting to control him. A second later Nick put on his device's headphones switching them on. This allowed him to cut out any audio distractions. He saw the cop's gun was still at the officer's feet and he quickly kicked it away.

"Man, we need our costumes," Charlie said.

The windows inside the van had started to fog up and they all wiped at the glass to see clearer.

"Look!" Fat Kid pointed into the sky.

They stared up into the night sky and saw Rachel Brooks dressed in her white vampire gown. She was flying over the chaotic scene below.

"Holy moly, it's Brooks," Henry said smiling.

"How'd she get her costume?" Fat Kid wondered out loud.

"Five finger discount no doubt," Charlie said bitterly. Henry elbowed his brother and Charlie elbowed him back.

They watched as Rachel flew down and landed like a dove on the street behind Fish. Fish's attention seemed to be drawn to Nick who stood like a fool with some homemade equipment in his hands. Those power lines were sparking now and even with Nick's rubber soled boots he would be fried like a Lloyd's chicken dinner – *crispy*!

"That guys is nuts," Charlie said.

"Or brave," Horatio mumbled, wishing he had that same bravery without his super suit.

"Damn Tom. We could be helping if he hadn't lost the footlocker."

Charlie sat back scowling.

"Tom didn't lose it. Whatever that black stuff is stole it, just like they stole the Borden Hatchet," Henry surmised.

Fat Kid watched helpless as his new friend, the friend that saved him from the same inky blackness in the alley, was going to get killed. Rachel Brooks was out there now too, but who knew what good she could do against this evil? Horatio looked back at Fish who was now lifting off the ground. His eyes were doing more than just glowing green, now they seemed to blast out in some gooey green substance. It dripped from his eyes as he hovered in the air and turned to face Rachel.

"Rachel no!"

Before he knew what he was doing Horatio was slipping into the driver seat of the VW van and cranking it over.

"Fat Kid what are you doing?" Charlie stared awed as he saw Horatio start the van and then drop it into drive. The van sped forward and Charlie and his brother flew backward.

In the air outside of the van the molecules took on a charged feel. Nick felt it crisp along his exposed flesh. He was reminded of the burnt toast he had had for breakfast yesterday. Switching on The Hose caused an immediate reaction from the Fish-thing. It had been turning slowly to face Rachel, who seemed like the primary threat. Now it twisted around to face Nick. Nick lifted the end of

The Hose and switched on the *extreme suck* function. A second later Fish-thing was pulled to the Earth and dragged toward The Hose. It screamed and growled, sounding like a possessed mountain lion.

Rachel lifted into the air and flew to the tormented power cables. She snagged them and yanked them from the transformer above. The sparks stopped sparking and she flew down still carrying the cables in her hands.

The VW van was speeding forward and stopped a foot from the Fish-thing as the creature was pulled toward The Hose. Fat Kid jumped out of the van and ran over to Rachel who was now grounded holding the cables. Henry and Charlie watched him exit the van but they stayed put. The wind had picked up and they also felt the molecules inside the van warm up.

"What the heck?" Henry said feeling like his exposed flesh was getting sunburned.

Charlie looked at his own hands and saw the usual pale flesh start to redden. They both stared out the window and saw the black cloud start to recede from Fish. The green glowing goo in his eyes dropped to the pavement as Nick sucked it into his canvas bag.

"Look at that," Charlie pointed into the sky.

The blackness lifted off him dropping Fish who was currently unconscious and it seemed to want to flee.

"Yeah!" Henry shouted as he and Charlie fist bumped each other.

But then the cloud seemed to take a form and shot toward Nick who lifted the Brainbuster. He was about to activate the device when the black cloud stopped its attack and then just dropped like dust to the street. There it collected and formed the monkey again. They all watched fascinated at this strange display.

"It's the monkey. It's Roscoe," Fat Kid said watching it walk on its hands toward Nick.

Fish was still out cold on the street in front of them. The green goo had almost completely cleared from his eyes now. Nick looked back at the monkey for a minute and that's when the monkey leapt onto his chest, snatched the Brainbuster and fled.

"Stop him!" Nick screamed as the monkey quickly sprinted down the street and hooked right down the next street. Nick was racing after him when Rachel took to the air, but it was too late. The creature had vanished.

Chapter Six

Tom had retreated inside The Impossible Dreams. He locked the front doors and the basement door. He thought he would wash away his sorrows with a bottle Scotch. Tom had taken more than a swallow when he saw the shadows outside the large picture window of the thrift store. The old proprietor tried to con himself into believing that those shadows were just local flat-foots making their nightly rounds. But he wasn't convinced.

"How have you come back?"

Even though the girls' faces were nothing but black shadows Tom knew those faces better than his own. He and his wife Rose, bless her soul, had borne them, raised them. Michelle and Melissa – now forever referred to as The Hatchet Sisters – had once been the loves of his life. They now suffered an eternity in that terrible world, The Keys To The Kingdom. It was his fault. It was all of his research and crap. He *hated* himself for causing the eternal torment that his daughters now experienced.

Tom wiped at his wet eyes and downed a shot of Scotch glancing at those haunted floating faces outside of his window.

"Go away! Go back to that dark place where you came from. You're not my girls!"

Tom raged on, throwing his shot glass at the front of the store. It shattered against the brick wall.

"Daddy, we love you. We have brought presents," the haunted sisters echoed in his mind.

Tom closed his eyes. He couldn't look at what they had brought him. He knew of at least two deaths because of these things that posed as his beloved daughters. He couldn't imagine what they could be offering him as *gifts*. When the images of the slain children flashed across his mind Tom screamed, dropping to his knees, beating against his old wrinkled forehead.

"No! No! No! You will not make me see! NO!"

"See the seeds of your labors. See what you have unleashed on the world." The echoing childish voices tore at him like daggers.

Tom wept like an abandoned child, and then his mind flashed on the new Coffin Kids – Horatio, Rachel, Charlie and Henry Bokar.

"The footlocker? Where is that footlocker?"

He heard the demented childish giggles echo outside the window, as if those ghouls knew the answer to that very question. Tom stepped to the glass, wiping away grime and stared into the dark abyss of those horrible demonic faces. He may have forsaken his daughters and for that he would be eternally damned, but maybe he could save the city from the infecting darkness that flooded from the cracks in their reality.

Tom removed the only relic he still owned that had once been a gift from his wife Rose, the mother of their daughters, Melissa and Michelle. It was a heart shaped locket that Tom always wore around his wrinkled old neck. Inside the locket were the pictures of the girls as babies on one side of the heart, on the other was a wedding picture of she and Tom in their youths.

"Love?" Tom whispered, wondering if it could be that easy.

He heard the demonic laughs. They were in his mind. They knew what he was thinking before…

"You know," they said laughing. "Daddy come out and play. We have played with other children. We will play with more. We will find the *child*…"

But then they cut off. Tom sparked on that. He glanced up and saw that the two haunted figures had vanished.

"The child?" Tom said wondering what that meant.

#

"This is bad, very bad," Nick said.

"What's so bad about a monkey stealing your doo-dad?" Charlie asked.

"This is really, *really* bad," Nick said again.

"I'm confused on the whole *really bad* thing. What's really bad?" Henry asked.

"Okay, that doo-dad, as you call it, is a Brainbuster."

Nick noticed that Horatio and the Bokar Brothers didn't understand the term, and why should they, Nick invented it.

"Essentially, imagine a thousand atom bombs exploding at once inside the human brain," Nick said.

"Total annihilation," Charlie giggled.

"FOR ALL OF US!" Nick shouted. "The entire city, heck that, make it the world."

"Why would you build something like that?" Fat Kid asked.

"Well I'm not even sure it works, or if it does I'm not even sure it does what I claim it does," Nick said seeing the skepticism on their faces. "I mean it could, and if it does it's in the hands of a...whatever the heck that monkey is. I'm sure it doesn't have the human race in its good graces."

When they heard Fish groaning on the ground Nick ran to his friend and rolled him over.

"Fish man, are you okay?"

Nick noticed some green goo still in Fish's eyes and tried to wipe it out. Fish started coughing. Nick helped him sit up and Fish threw up all over himself. Charlie giggled and Henry elbowed him. Charlie elbowed his brother back.

"What happened?" Fish asked and then vomited again. Again Charlie chuckled.

"It was that darkness again. The one from the alley, and man...the monkey stole my Brainbuster," Nick said.

Fish wiped spit and vomit off his scruffy goatee chin and met his friend's eyes.

"We're outnumbered. We have to call *them*," Nick said.

Fish nodded his head defeated.

Fat Kid stepped forward.

"Call who?"

#

Old Dogg was leaning back in his wooden swivel chair smoking a cigar reading the racing forms when he received the call. It had been slow for The Clock Strikes Ten ghost buster unit most of the week. Dogg thought that with the kid deaths there would be some ghost business. Most of the Clock Strikes Ten crew were out of town on other missions. At least that's what he told himself. The crew had a thing about regrouping in DenMark in the month of October though when many of the spook, specters, and ghosts lurked the city streets striking fear into the DenMark citizens. But none of them had returned.

"Yeah, Clock Strikes Ten, 'You gotta ghost, we gotta answer.' What can I do fer ya?" Dogg said into the telephone.

"Dogg, is that you?"

Dogg almost swallowed his cigar when he heard the young guy's voice on the other line. He took another moment to recover before he spoke.

"Nicholas? That you?"

"Yeah, it's me Dogg. We need your help," Nick said.

"*We*? Am I to believe that you is still hanging with that loser Fish? Boy, ain't you got the sense God give you? I told ya to leave that bum and come back to werk fer me. We kickin' it lately."

Dogg looked around at the empty station and groaned.

"Could use yer inventions. Got anythin' the old Dogg could use?"

"That's what I'm calling about. Has the band picked up any unusual PKE readings around the city over the last twenty-four hours?"

"PKE readings? Well, just between the two of us, most of the gang's outta town. Just me and Mel in right now. Other fellas oughta be back in town by the end of the week. Why?"

"We got trouble, right here in DenMark city," Nick said feeling like he was about to go into a dancing and singing routine from the musical, The Music Man.

"Trouble, eh? Where you at?"

"Graham's Town Hall Theater lot. We were attacked by something enormous. Black ectoplasm all over the place. Fish…Fish was possessed," Nick whispered this last bit.

"Possessed? What level we talkin' kid?"

"Off the charts. Best guess we're looking at a Spiritus, or a Fright, but a damned big one. Can you help?"

After a second of thought old Dogg nodded to himself.

"Yeah, sure. Give me a little bit. I'll be in touch. You at the same digits?"

"Same," Nick said.

"Be talkin' soon. And Nicholas?"

"Yeah?"

"Good ta hear from ya boy. Real good."

"You too Dogg," Nick said killing the line.

112

After he hung up Dogg looked at the black telephone for a long time as he chewed on his cigar.

"Off the charts? Couldn't be," he said thinking about old Tom at The Impossible Dreams Thrift Store. "You old geezer, what are you up to now?"

#

After hearing the demonic girls mention a *child* Tom started pulling books that he knew of that dealt with demonic children. If the child they were talking about was demonic, like them, then based off the literature it said that most demonic children were spawned from high-level entities, or demons.

"These children are pure evil, demonic beings and have no soul. Soulless?"

Tom started thinking again. He knew about the wheel of fate. How the wheel always came back around to expose the good, bad, and ugly of life and the after-life. Tom's demons were literally coming back to haunt him now. If the Hatchet Sisters were searching for a demonic child what could that mean?

Tom thought about the growing darkness that was leaking out of the dimension, The Keys To The Kingdom. He started thinking of Winkie Witch on Bradbury Street, and now the Hatchet Sisters. His modest attempts at repairing the damage to the walls of reality that he started in his youth had not worked. He would need to contact more of his former Coffin Kids. Nick and Fish were now back in the fold. Tom wanted to call The Clock Strikes Ten station on Peko, but the way he had left things with Dogg Johnson, well he thought maybe he would give the Death Strides a call first.

Pulling out his rolodex he flipped to D's.

#

The Death Strides ghost buster team - Barb, Patty, and Tammy were all loading up. Barb had just slipped on her fingerless leather gloves and Patty and her younger sister, Tammy, were pulling on their trademark studded leather jackets. They were a relic of the 1980's punk, tough, girl-band era. Not only were these three chicks kick-butt ghost hunters but they also were a thrashing punk metal band that played gigs throughout the city.

Tonight they were playing a late-night gig at an old slaughterhouse named Pete's Pig Butchery. It was way down on the east end of the city in no-where's-ville. But the girls needed the money. Tammy said that she had a line on some new hardware that would up their ghost hunting game. Besides, the tools could be cool instruments for

114

their band too, she said bashfully. Tammy was the youngest, and smartest, of the band. Patty was the oldest and wisest. Barb was in middle, but she was the undisputed leader. Her wavy blonde-platinum hair was more than just a relic of the 80's, it was a force to be reckoned with. Together they were, The Death Strides. No one messed with these chicks. They were like a collective bulldozer.

Back in the day there were three ghost hunter teams. The Clock Strikes Ten, which were comprised primarily of blue-collared men working every job they could get no matter how crappy the gigs were just to keep food on the table. These were the lowest of the low. They still ran a small station on Peko with Duct Tape and a prayer. The second group was The Death Strides, composed of only women. These girls were tougher than any guy and ruled most of the pricier gigs. They also started a punk heavy metal band and kept with it. The band was their primary source of income. They were loved in Europe. The third ghost hunter team took on only corporate jobs. They were sleek and professional with a mysterious edge that none of the other groups had. Their name? The Dream Police. They owned an entire high rise in the Park Avenue area of DenMark. Their client list was nothing shy of the elite of the city.

The Death Strides were loading into their van when Barb's cell phone buzzed. She unzipped her fanny pack and answered it.

"Barb here, speak!"

Patty was in the driver seat and Tammy was buckling into the back bench seat. They both watched Barb speak. Patty waited to crank over the van until Barb finished her talk. When the blonde killed the line she sat silent for a minute.

"Who was it?" Patty asked.

"Old Tom," Barb said simply.

"*Tom*, Tom?" Patty asked.

Barb nodded. The van remained silent for a long time. They each knew what the others were thinking. All three had worked for Tom as young girls. All three had seen the evil that had been knocking, two doors down. And all three had left Tom because they believed that the old guy was marked for death. Still, he was the reason that they had become ghost hunters, fighting to retain the light of the world.

"What did he want?" Tammy asked from the back seat.

"He needs our help. Said that something's entered our world that even *he's* never seen before," Barb said. Her tough chin quivered as she spoke.

"What about the gig at the slaughterhouse?" Patty asked.

"What about our lives?" Tammy asked sounding frightened.

A cold expression passed over their leader's face. It was a look the Schneider Sisters had seen before. It meant it was time to take care of business.

"It's what we do. Hit it Pat," Barb commanded.

Patty dropped the van into drive and they roared out.

#

Dogg and Mel arrived at the Graham's Town Hall Theater parking lot where Nick, Fish and the boys were waiting. Rachel was still in the sky searching for a possible location to where the monkey could have fled. Fish had retired to the cab of Flo the VW van while Henry and Charlie were discussing the merits of the DenMark street vendor's hotdogs and hoagies with Fat Kid. Nick was pacing nervously waiting for his former employer to arrive and help them. He hadn't seen

Dogg in a couple of years. He and Fish had kept their ghost hunting on the down low trying not to disturb their former team, The Clock Strikes Ten.

When the large black man exited the old Hearse, which was Dogg's ghost hunting vehicle of choice, he had the biggest, friendliest smile that Nick could ever have hoped for. They embraced as Dogg blew out a smog of cigar smoke.

"Good to see you Dogg," Nick said.

"You too kid. Where's yer partner?"

Nick motioned to the old VW Van where Fish was seated in the front seat looking white as a ghost.

Dogg walked over to the van and knocked on the window, motioning for Fish to roll it down. Fish obliged.

"Damn son, you look like a level ten entity just crawled up yer poop chute," Dogg said grinning.

"I smell that you're still smoking those rancid cigars," Fish said waving the smoke away. He then looked at Nick. "See you're the cavalry. Such as it is."

Fish looked up and down Dogg once in a most disgusted way. They obviously did not get along.

"Cavalry's me and Mel," Dogg said pointing at his partner, a young female dressed in a pair of black coveralls with The Clock Strikes Ten logo on the breast pocket. She was chewing a piece of gum like it was going out of style. Her face had bits of grease smeared across its pretty features.

"Still a stellar mechanic?" Fish asked scornfully.

Mel just smiled at the dude and walked over to Flo, the VW Van.

"Pop the hood," she said.

Fish looked to Nick who nodded. The boys all stepped forward to watch this interaction. Fish popped the hood. Besides her black ghost hunter jump suit Mel carried a utility belt with a dozen tools, most covered with grease.

She took one look at the engine and shook her head pulling out a wrench and then stepped up onto the bumper.

"Hey now!"

Fish slid out from inside the van and started toward Mel but Nick stopped him for a minute. They watched the young woman work. She went through the engine like she had every inch of it memorized. Charlie was blushing at this young woman as she worked. He stepped up to within elbow's reach and leaned forward to see what she was adjusting. Henry pulled him back just before the woman's elbow struck Charlie's face. She was working and no one messed with Mel when she was under a hood.

They all watched her work. Dogg had a massive pleased grin on his face as he puffed off his cigar. When Mel finished she slammed the hood down wiping grease on an old rag that dangled from her back pocket.

"Start 'er up," she said.

Fish stared at Mel and Dogg curiously but slid into the driver seat and started the engine. It ran like a dream, quiet as any new automobile. Mel just smirked her approval. Fish looked angry and Fat Kid, well Fat Kid was floored.

"Wow. That junker sounded like it was about to fall apart an hour ago," Fat Kid said.

"Could use an oil change, and fluids topped off but, yeah she runs okay, with a woman's touch," Mel said winking at the boys. They all blushed.

"Yeah well…just keep your distance. Flo's our jalopy," Fish said defiantly.

"So back to bizness. Mel and me got some supplies that might help ya. I suspect that old Nick here's got some of his own, but Mel's been dabblin' in the invention trade as well," Dogg said proudly.

He led the others around the back of the rusted old Hearse and opened the creaking load in door. Dogg hit a switch on the side of the Hearse and an overhead light flickered on. There were cleanly placed tools of varying design latched down securely along the walls and bed of the vehicle.

"Wow," Fat Kid said again as he and the Bokar Brothers peered in.

"Nick, who these kids?" Dogg asked pointing at Horatio, Charlie, and Henry.

"They're some of Tom's new recruits. Call them Coffin Kids 2.0."

Dogg cocked a cynical bushy eyebrow and Nick just shrugged.

"I figured that old fella'd be behind this. Guy's cursed," Dogg said.

"That *old fella* is the one who got us into our work. And to be honest I like what we do. It's helping people, helping the city we call home," Nick said.

Old Dogg looked long and hard at Nick and then let out a belly laugh.

"That's good and all as long as old Tom keeps his distance because this old dog's not getting sucked into his baggage."

Dogg was still smiling but Nick saw the hurt in the man's brown eyes. Things had gone bad between Tom and Dogg. Neither ever wanted to discuss it. Nick didn't like to press sensitive subjects so he let it drop.

"Well, anyway. here's what we have so far."

Nick showed Dogg his readings from the black ectoplasm cloud and again Dogg almost swallowed his cigar. The expression on his face frightened Nick. It was telling, as if Nick could see secrets floating up from some dark abyss in the man's soul.

"Dogg what is it?"

They had all gathered around the large black man now. Dogg looked down at most of them. Fish was about an inch taller than Dogg. After a long pause the constipated expression on Dogg's face changed to terror and Fish asked what they all wanted to know.

"Well, Dogg what's the deal dude?"

"That old fool. That damned *fool*," Dogg said.

Charlie looked at the others for a second and then stepped up to Dogg.

"What's the old *fool* done?"

"He's killed us all..."

Chapter Seven

Somewhere in time a small child slept. It was late after all. After midnight the boy, Tom, slept in his bed with his bear and honey sheets pulled up to his neck. He snored softly. His blonde hair was the color of honey, like Pooh's porcelain pot. Tom believed in Pooh, his own Pooh not the chubby bear that stumbled about like a stew bum. Just then Tom was dreaming about his Pooh, or Pooka.

Here in this place in his dreams Tom and his Pooka, Barlow were together. Barlow was a duck; actually he was a Pooka who shape shifted into a green mallard duck in a brown rumpled corduroy suit. The Pooka waited night after night for the boy to appear, the special boy who made things happen. That boy was expected tonight. Tonight was a big one for Tom.

The beings beyond had tapped through quicker than Barlow or any of the others had suspected.

The knock echoed on the door of the cubicle apartment.

"That's my boy," Barlow whispered with glee.

The mallard waddled to the door and opened the cubicle door. The small boy with the honey blonde hair stepped inside.

"You made it. *Excelente*!"

Barlow flapped his wings welcoming the boy inside.

"Hi," Tom said quietly.

"So what would you like to do tonight boy? Trips on the high sea, or maybe we could wrangle some bison on the prairies. No, no I have it. OUTERSPACE!"

"Oh, I don't know," Tom said.

He sounded more glum than normal.

"For a chap who's got the world at his fingertips you're awfully depressed. Are you depressed Tom?"

The boy glanced up at the mallard.

"You said my name."

"Of course," Barlow said.

"But normally you call me, boy, or chap, or kid, but you just called me Tom now. Why?"

"Because…because, well it's your name isn't it?"

"I guess," the boy said staring around the mallard's cubicle size apartment.

It was congested inside this place and Tom often wondered why he came here in his dreams. He had been coming here since as far back as he could remember. Two doors down he often heard a group that Barlow called The Party Club. He said that they were laughing and drinking and having a party. Tom said that he loved parties but Barlow warned that the boy needed to stay away from this party. When asked why, the mallard just squawked at him. Tom didn't like to be squawked at so he never asked about The Party Club again.

Tonight things seemed quiet.

Tom could feel that Barlow was anxious about something. Like using the boy's name. Barlow never did that. Something was wrong. Tom didn't want this strange awkwardness here in his special dreamscape, he had enough of that in the real world.

"What's wrong duck?"

"Wrong? Wrong, nothing wrong. Why would you think anything was wrong?"

"I don't know. You just kinda seem, different, nervous."

Tom stared at Barlow who couldn't meet his eyes. Then the duck smiled with his long yellow beak and removed something from behind his back. At first Tom couldn't understand what he was looking at.

"It's a block of wood?" Tom said.

"Nope, have a look," Barlow said setting the wooden item on the floor.

Tom got a better look now. It wasn't a block of wood at all. It was a footlocker.

"What's that for?"

"Open it up and see," Barlow said.

Tom dropped to his knees in front of the footlocker and opened the latch.

"What's inside?"

"Reach in."

But Tom felt that strange anxiety pulsing off the duck again. Why was Barlow acting so weird?

"REACH IN THE BOX BOY!"

The voice was not his Pooka's voice. The voice was…

Tom shot awake grabbing for the wooden footlocker. He was sweating. He glanced around the shop. He must have fallen asleep sometime after calling the Death Strides. A second later a rap on the front door made him jump. He stumbled out of his chair and peered over the counter toward the front door. He saw three shadows standing there looking in.

"Tom! Come on open the door."

He heard the familiar barking voice of Barb Bigby, leader of the Death Strides.

"Old Tom you're getting too old for this stuff," he said as he exited the counter and walked to the front of the shop.

After unlocking the front door he let the ladies inside with a smile.

"It's cold out there. What took you so long? We were beating on the door for almost five minutes," Barb said irritably pushing her way into the store.

"Same old Barb," Tom said half joking.

Barb turned on him. She was quite a sight in her leather slacks, sleeveless denim jacket and studded gloves. The other girls were dressed similarly in studded leather. The look went with their thrashing band. When they played gigs they were hardcore and tonight was no exception.

"Yeah *same* old Barb," she snarled.

"Besides Tom you called us. What do you want?" Patty said.

She was taller and slimmer than the rest. Her long straight brown hair dangled in her pale face making her look like a Goth chick. Her ruby red lips accentuated the dead look to her corpse-pale complexion.

Tammy stood quietly behind the others. She played the drums in their band but never seemed to fit in, with her short stature and frizzy dark hair. Her complexion was also much tanner and clearer than the other two band members.

"That I did, and with good reason too. Follow me," Tom said as he started toward the back of the store.

"No *way*," Barb said. "We're not going anywhere with you old man. Put up or shut up."

Tom stopped, turned and looked at these three young women. They had once been part of his Coffin Kids entourage when they were in their early teens. Barb was always the most belligerent one. Patty was the most aloof, and Tammy, well Tammy was just quiet.

"Okay little lady. Here's the gist. In a nutshell the world as we know it will end if you don't help me repair some cracks in reality. Beyond those cracks is the astral world of monsters and demons. I'm not gonna insult your intelligences by explaining more about that. I know about your ghost hunting exploits. I will tell you that years ago I *accidently* tapped a dark world known by the mystics as – The Keys To The Kingdom. If any more of that evil escapes, we're through – Earth, the human race EVERYTHING!"

They all stood silent for a minute processing this news and then Barb spoke.

"If this is so vital then why didn't you just call corporate? The Dream Police have more sway than the rest of us as far as ghost busting goes. If this danger is really as bad as you say they have a stock in stopping it too."

130

Tom shook his head removing his beat up old Fedora and wiped at the sweat that had gathered along his scalp.

"It's not that easy," Tom said.

"Why? Why's it not that easy," Patty asked.

He didn't answer right away, but when Barb and Patty started to ask again he shouted at them.

"Because they no longer take my calls."

The Death Strides all looked at one another, shocked, but Barb quickly recovered with her trademark sarcasm.

"I'm not surprised. I mean what you put George through...well, I wouldn't take your calls either," Barb said.

Tammy stepped forward seeing that the old man was already beaten. Tammy took Tom's hand and looked up into his watery eyes.

"How can we patch this up?"

"Tam..." Patty started but Tammy turned on her sister.

"It's what we do," Tammy snarled back.

Barb and Patty just stared at each other shocked.

"Tell us. How do we stop this evil?" Tammy asked.

Tom looked at them for a minute and then just shrugged.

#

"Are you telling us that Old Tom started all of this evil?" Nick sounded doubtful.

The Bokar Brothers seemed to be taking this seriously. They had done some more than morally questionable *Turns* for Tom in the past and knew that the old fella had a dark spot. Fat Kid just sat quietly taking it all in.

"Look at us," Dogg said pointing at the small band – Nick, Fish, Mel, Henry and Charlie Bokar, and Horatio. "We've all been recruited by that old bird. We've all been put in harm's way on more than one occasion. Heck, Tom's not much of a father. I mean he dangled his own daughters, Michelle and Melissa, in front of the gates of The Keys To The Kingdom for crying out loud."

"That was a mistake," Fat Kid said.

They all looked at the eleven year old pudgy kid. Horatio Patterson had a soft way about him but when he spoke he could be persuasive.

"What do you mean?" Nick asked.

"I mean Tom didn't know that he was opening the gates of Hell, or whatever you call this evil place. I mean you are assuming he's done all of this because he's cursed, and maybe he is cursed, but he brought us all in over the years to battle this evil. I think that means something...doesn't it?"

Mel looked up at Dogg, who looked at Nick, who in turn looked at Fish. Henry walked up to Fat Kid and clamped him on the chubby shoulder.

"Well spoken, Horatio," Henry said.

"Yeah Fat Kid, good speech but where does that leave us," Charlie said.

"Obviously we need to get back to The Impossible Dreams and..." Nick started to say but Dogg cut him off.

"Wait just a minute, let's not start jumpin' the gun fellas. I said I'd come and help *you*," Dogg said pointing at Nick. "I didn't say nothin' about helpin' Tom."

"Don't look at it as helping Tom. Look at it as saving the world," Horatio said.

He was eager to help old Tom though. They could say what they wanted about the old proprietor of The Impossible Dreams but Horatio respected Tom. Horatio had become part of a team now. He wasn't the kind of kid that had many friends. Everyone makes mistakes, some worse than others, but at the end of the day friends and family are there to pull you out of the fire. Right now Tom was burning up and Horatio meant to put him out of the flames.

Dogg squinted at Fat Kid for a minute.

"Yer dad a politician, kid?" Dogg asked.

"Nah, he's a logger." Fat Kid just blushed.

Dogg burst into a loud barrel laugh that infected all of them. Charlie elbowed Henry and rolled his eyes like that big black dude was nuts. Henry nodded, but then they both burst into laughter.

"Okay so let's load up. Destination, Impossible Dreams," Fish said tossing aside his cigarette and sliding into the front seat of Flo, the VW van.

Henry and Charlie ran to the van pushing each other aside looking for the shotgun seat. Nick quickly brushed them aside and then opened the door. He would be riding shotgun. The Bokar Brothers slid in the back but Fat Kid hesitated staring up into the night sky.

"What is it Horatio?" Nick asked.

"Rachel. Rachel is up there somewhere in all that darkness," he said pointing into the starry sky.

They all glanced up.

#

Rachel soared through the night sky. She loved the feel of the wind on her now undead flesh. The stars were bright tonight and with her vampire eyes she could see for miles. Initially she scanned the city blocks surrounding the last known location of the dark cloud that was the colorful monkey. When she saw nothing unusual she widened her search to the outer streets of the city and ultimately to the dark trees of the DenMark Park.

She remembered the last time she was out on this dirt road she was kidnapped by Winkie Witch riding in her black coach. Horatio was flying after them in his super hero suit that night, but the witch caught him by surprise and shot him with her twisted magic wand.

Tonight though, she, Rachel, was the creature of the night with all the power of an adult vampire queen. Now she did not fear the dark but embraced it. The books in her mother's trailer, the ones that her mother's beau saw and accused her of being a witch, had been her solace over the last year as their little band had broken up. She hadn't spoken to Horatio much at school or otherwise, but she wanted to. She knew that he did too.

In her bedroom, locked away from the depressing world Rachel began to study, not her school work but the art of magic. Once exposed to the items in Tom's Impossible Dreams, she was unable to not go further in exploring what other magical relics lay waiting. Rachel checked out as many books as she could from the DenMark Public Library on witchcraft and the occult, trying not to draw unwanted attention. One book talked about alternate dimensions where entities, good and evil, existed. Some of these entities existed on the same plane, but depending on how one approached that plane it would open to the good or the evil entities.

Rachel felt that perhaps this was the ultimate test of character.

Maybe it was her tough upbringing not having a father figure, but instead having a mother who had boyfriends hanging around the trailer at all hours of the night. But Rachel began to succumb to the depressive states in her mind. She would be okay for a long time but then would feel like tearing the world apart with *rage*. She began to wonder if she was in fact a hero like the others or if maybe she was simply…bad. Hadn't the magical footlocker given her an evil undead blood sucking creature? Horatio got the super hero suit, and it fitted him to a T. Horatio was most definitely a super hero. He was kind and generous. He cared for his friends and was selfless. Rachel wasn't like him, as much as she loved…*loved*? – him.

It was true that Charlie and Henry Bokar were also saddled with monster characters, the werewolf and zombie, but they were scamps. Those creatures were not innately evil like the vampire. The werewolf changed into a monster once a month, but lived a normal life the other days. The zombie, well the zombie was a resurrected corpse, mindless and hungry. There was no evil in that.

The more she thought on this as she flew through the night the more determined she was to find this darkness and confront it.

"What was that?"

Rachel saw the shadows that made up the bulk of the dark pine trees for the DenMark Park begin to move. Normally one might see the shadows move based off the wind blowing against the leaves but this was an independent movement. It was so bizarre. The shadows were blacker than any shadows Rachel had seen before.

"How brilliant," she said as the darkness seemed to rise from the trees as if using those trees for camouflage.

She watched as the darkness, maybe blackness was a better term, pulled away from the branches like some hidden predator having stalked its prey and now was ready to reveal itself. But Rachel glanced around and saw no prey. It wasn't until the blackness started moving away from the park in her direction that she realized that *she* was the prey.

Rachel flew higher into the air trying to get beyond the blackness's reach. She flew as fast as she could in the opposite direction not knowing where she was going, but the dark shadows were everywhere and they were lifting into the sky like a giant net. Fear streaked through her then. She watched, hovering over the trees, as the black net lifted and started to overtake her. Something inside Rachel Brooks retreated watching the black folds of that net encircle her and then cinch up. She was

138

within their grasp now. Now she would be truly tested on her character. This was her last thought as the black world around her embraced her and vanished.

#

"This ain't good," Dogg said when he saw the Death Strides van parked in front of The Impossible Dreams Thrift Store.

He and Mel exchanged a disgusted look.

Fish knocked on the passenger window of the Hearse and Mel rolled it down.

"What are you waiting for old man?"

"You see that van," Dogg pointed at the Death Strides van with the painting of a killer female bass player thrashing a demon splashed across the side.

Fish and Nick both looked at the van.

"Damn," Fish said. He and Nick both knew about the female ghost hunting team, The Death Strides. They were the baddest women in the city.

When Fish and Nick worked for The Clock Strikes Ten group The Death Strides were always one step ahead. It seemed like things hadn't changed.

"So what do we do now?" Fish asked.

Flo's side door slid back and the Bokar Brothers exited followed by Fat Kid. They started toward the front of the shop when Dogg shouted for them to stop.

"Hey boys, where ya goin'?"

"Inside," Charlie said smirking like Dogg's question was the stupidest thing he had ever heard.

"Not with that van parked out front."

The boys looked at the cool van with the killer paint job.

"The Death Strides? What's that?" Henry asked.

"You mean *who's* that. They the nastiest female ghost hunters that this city done turned out. They werked fer Tom a few years back. Nasty, nothin' but nasty," Dogg said grinding his teeth.

"So what? We just gonna hang here like a bunch of whipped losers?" Charlie asked and then started toward the front of the store when they all saw it happen.

All eyes shifted when they heard the un-godly howl in the alley next to Impossible Dreams. At

140

first Fat Kid thought it was an alley cat but as the howl grew it sounded more like a demonic mountain lion.

"Get back in here kids!" Nick was sliding from the VW van now pulling at The Hose he still had clamped to his belt.

Charlie was closer to the front door of the thrift store and raced to it. Henry backed away from the growing blackness. He bumped into Horatio who grabbed Henry by the wrist and pulled him back to the van. Fat Kid glanced back at the Hearse as Dogg and Mel were slipping out of it. They ran around to the back of the Hearse's loading door and were pulling out their ghost hunter equipment as the blackness attacked.

The cloud created a giant spiked fist and the fingers wrapped around Dogg's ankle, lifting him into the air. Nick stepped forward switching on The Hose which caused the black cloud to scream with rage. It turned part of its attention to Nick swatting at the ghost hunter. Nick dodged the swipe and rolled aside. Fish was still staring up into the vacant blackness looking like maybe he was about to wet his pants when Horatio snagged him and pushed him forward toward the front of The Impossible Dreams store.

Charlie was already beating at the front door when Horatio, Henry, and Fish arrived. Tom was staring out through the grimy glass.

"Tom, open up man!" Charlie screamed not looking back at the growing chaos.

Tom threw open the door but instead of him allowing them to run inside the shop he and three leather clad chicks exited.

"Who the heck are you?" Charlie asked looking at the three chicks.

The girls all stepped forward flaunting their leather garbs throwing back their hair.

"We're the Death Strides," Barb said pulling on her fingerless gloves.

"You mean the *dead strides*-- look out!" Horatio shouted as he saw one of the black cloud's giant fists swipe at the female band. They easily side stepped the fist and made it to their van sliding open the side door.

Tammy jumped inside and immediately switched on her ghost hunter computer system. Patty snagged their ghost hunter weapons and tossed Barb her favorite a vintage Sterling guitar. The guitar was an import from an undisclosed country, that didn't exist on any current maps, and with its musical strings it created a resonance that helped isolate and capture almost any type of entity imaginable.

The Sterling flashed silver in Barb's hands as she strummed a few notes.

"These chicks are wacked," Charlie said giggling.

Henry nodded as he watched the Death Strides weapon up. They didn't show a sign of fear in the face of this encroaching black ectoplasmic cloud. He had to hand it to them, they were brave chicks.

Dogg was still in the grip of the black cloud fist as Mel pulled out a small tool that looked kind of like a wrench. She was so short and small in front of the giant fisted cloud that anyone looking might have thought she was a child. But, unlike Dogg who was a large man screaming like a baby now, Mel simply twisted a scale on the wrench and a bright blue light shot out from the tool and seized the black fist. Dogg dropped to the ground moaning as the fist froze like a block of ice. Mel tapped it with a small hammer she held in her coveralls and the iced cloud shattered into a million fragments.

"Wow," Fat Kid said watching the Mel work.

"Get inside boys," Tom pushed them into the store.

"Wait, I gotta see this," Charlie was saying but Horatio and Henry were dragging him inside The Impossible Dreams shop.

Once inside Tom locked the door and drew the blinds.

"Tom, what the heck are you doing man?" Charlie said.

"Chuck, hold up. That thing, whatever it is out there is looking to eat all of us. We're not equipped to deal with this, not without our costumes," Henry said.

"Yeah Tom, what about those costumes? Where the heck are they?" Charlie was in Tom's face now.

They all watched as the old man quivered away from them and the darkness out front. After a long quiet moment as the small group inside the store listened to the horror that was happening outside Horatio finally turned back to Tom.

"Tom where's the footlocker?"

Tom looked at them for a second and just shrugged.

"Great!" Charlie said.

Even Henry was angry at Tom now. The world might be coming to an end outside and their hands were tied.

"We gotta do something. There has to be something magical in this place we can use. Come on Hank," Charlie said as he walked down one of the aisles. Henry hesitated and then followed his brother.

Horatio stood by the door listening to the screams outside as he watched Tom who seemed to have gone catatonic. He had never seen an adult look like that in his whole eleven years on the planet and he didn't like it.

"Tom, you think that the footlocker was stolen, like the hatchet?"

"The hatchet? Yeah the hatchet, the footlocker? Oh, Horatio my boy I could kiss your chubby cheeks. I remember having a dream before the hatchet went missing, before the footlocker disappeared. I had a dream about a boy I knew..." he paused closing his eyes trying to envision the dream.

Horatio tried to be patient but with the screams outside and the Bokar Brothers yelling at each other as they ran up and down the aisles things were becoming insane.

"Tom, the boy? Who is the boy?"

Tom opened his eyes and looked at Fat Kid.

"*Me*, I'm the boy, or was a long time ago…a *very* long time ago. I once visited a place, well more than once, every night as a child. I would visit a safe place. This place always welcomed me. My best friend was a…oh god, *Barlow*!"

Fat Kid watched the old man as tears ran down Tom's wrinkled cheeks. Oh brother, Tom had lost his mind, finally after all these years the old fella had gone batty. Horatio turned away from Tom and started for the front door.

#

Industrial. Smog. Burnt electrical wiring. Giggles. Cries. Laughs. Chants. Screams – these are the impressions I have every night at midnight when I hear the Party Club two doors down, laughing and drinking and having a party. Every night is the same. Industrial. Smog. Burnt electrical wiring. Giggles. Cries. Laughs. Chants. Screams. Laughing and drinking and having a party. I used to work. I can't work anymore because the Party Club rings in my mind. Laughing and drinking and having a party two doors down. I don't go out anymore, except to sit next to their door, two doors down laughing and drinking and having a party. The stink of industrial metal. The laughs of deranged teens. The smell of sweating leather. The sound of scratching along vinyl. These are the sounds of the Party Club. It started as an irritation, then became a frustrated rally for sanity. Now, now it's an obsession. I no longer am a prisoner of my cubicle. Now I am a prisoner of their cubicle. Their sounds. Their smells. Their laughter, grunts, moans. I watch them through my key hole. Some come in. Some go out. They wear leather. Maybe that is their skin – rough, torn leather. The faces are undefined. I started wearing leather. I stopped shaving. I'm whipped now. When they first arrived they frightened me. Now I fear I can't live without them and their horrible jeers. I saw them move a short circuit monitor in their cubicle apartment. What's that for? Who are they watching? Can I watch? I have popcorn. I have leather. Sitting outside their door I whistle, 'Two doors down, laughing and drinking and having a party…'

How long had she been here in this forgotten cubicle-like apartment listening to the mad Party Club? Somehow the where was obvious: 91 Greene.

But what was 91 Greene? And then her memory reasserted itself and she remembered being consumed by the black cloud from the DenMark Park. She was still wearing her vampire gown and still felt the magic pulse inside her, only now the power felt different, stronger. Inside this black ectoplasm she felt as though the true nature of her powers were fully realized. It was insane but Rachel Brooks finally felt home.

Everything shifted then and the Party Club with the stink of burnt electricity and giggles vanished. Now she was standing among many shadows in a palace sized space. Large vault ceilings with great splayed buttresses crisscrossing them were above her head. There was a gleaming object on the mantle before her.

Rachel felt the nightmare beings that populated the space rather than saw them now. Their eager eyes bore into her like hot coals. Rachel did not dare look around but instead she focused her vision on the metal object on the mantle before her. She was within just a few feet when she realized what it was – a glowing metal hatchet. The shaft of the hatchet was ancient looking wrapped leather. As Rachel approached it she realized that she was unconsciously floating like a magnet toward the metal of the hatchet.

148

"Wow," she whispered as she now stood within reach of the pulsing hatchet.

All the power that had flooded her on her arrival at 91 Greene, wherever this place was, paled in comparison to the power she felt pulsing off this metal object. Rachel suspected that the material used for this hatchet wasn't the kind of metal that was forged on Earth. There was something more than molecular elements that made up this hatchet. She felt a consciousness drawing her hand forward. It was a consciousness inside the hatchet, an intelligence all its own.

When Rachel touched the leather shaft of the hatchet a million memories of a million other wielders flooded her consciousness. She saw ancient times on Earth when prehistoric man wielded the hatchet as something special giving the wielder authority over all his brethren. Then there were memories of Atlantis before it sank into the sea. The Egyptians came next followed by the Middle Ages. She even watched as Medieval Knights swung the hatchet bringing down their enemies. Lizzie Borden was one of the last memories. The horror that had once started with pride in the relic now was all consuming. For the last two centuries Rachel felt the evil that had latched onto the once heroic weapon grow. Now another memory - this one was of a boy with blonde hair. Time sped forward exposing the boy as a young man, and then an old man and finally…

"Tom," Rachel whispered.

She saw how Tom started exploring the darkness outside of the walls of reality, how he knocked and those dark nightmares answered, and how he had spent decades trying to make amends with his generations of Coffin Kids. The footlocker was also something that had been fashioned and handed down to him by some unseen entities. As much as Rachel searched the hatchet's memories whoever, or whatever made the footlocker was not there.

For now that didn't matter. What did matter was the power that she felt surging through her. It was so much power that Rachel knew that she could never return to her normal life in the trailer park with her mother and her mother's beaus. The strength that the hatchet gave her made her vampire gown fell like a cheap dime store costume.

As Rachel lifted the hatchet into the air and a blinding shot of light illuminated the darkness she heard hisses and screams from the encroaching nightmares. She turned for the first time and flashed the steel of the hatchet blade at the darkness. Many of the beings were merely dark clouds. Once the light hit them they vanished. Rachel wasn't sure if it was the feeling of scaring off the nightmares she enjoyed or if it was the power over them that excited her more.

She wondered where Horatio and the others were? Was the city still in danger now that she had control of the magic hatchet that had caused the death of those poor children? Rachel knew that she needed to return to DenMark, but how did she escape the black cloud?

#

The black cloud had gotten larger and more belligerent as they fought it.

Tammy had warmed up the van. Inside of which was the Big'en. The Big'en was what the Death Strides called their all-encompassing entity snatching net. The Death Strides had captured over one thousand different entities in their time ghost hunting. They had saved, with an entire molecular breakdown, all of these entities in the database inside the van. Tammy, the genius, had used the molecular makeup of every entity they had ever encountered and created a cosmic net that shot from the back of the van with a simple spring and pulley system. The trick was lining up the entity.

At present Barb and Patty were trying like mad to hold the expanding black cloud at bay so that their sister in arms could line up the van and the net. Nick was still working on sucking up as much of the cloud as he could in The Hose but the canvas ecto bag was dangerously close to over-inflating and if that happened – KAPOW! Everything that he had sucked in would escape and it would be doubly mad.

He looked around but saw Fish nowhere in sight.

Dogg had strapped on an ecto-blaster pack and had switched it on. It felt like they had been battling for hours but Nick knew that it had barely been minutes since the black cloud appeared and attacked them. Mel had used her ecto freeze tool that she had always kept on her key chain. It worked great for quick escapes. Nick had been real proud when she invented that tool, and a little envious.

Now Dogg approached the black fist of the cloud racking an ecto blasting load into the chamber of his ecto-blaster. He fired just as the giant black fist was about to slam him into the earth. Nick was reminded of the massive green hands of the Incredible Hulk. When Dogg pulled the ecto-blaster trigger it felt like the entire Earth shook and a huge flash of light escaped the end of the barrel as the

152

black fist evaporated. The rest of the ectoplasmic cloud took notice of this blast and started to quickly withdraw back into the shadows where they bled from.

Mel started to cheer when one quick rattle snake-like shadow latched out and attached itself to her. Mel and Dogg exchanged a terrified looked and then she disappeared into the blackness and was gone. All of the shadows had vanished.

"NO! MEL!" Dogg screamed in his deep guttural voice, his cigar dropping to the wet pavement.

He let the nozzle for the ecto-blaster drop to the ground and drag along the pavement as he sprinted to the spot where Mel disappeared. He started to claw at the pavement until his fingers bled and then he stepped back and blasted several large holes into the black pavement with the ecto-blaster, but Mel was gone. The black cloud had swallowed her up whole.

The thing was quick. Nick shivered at the thought and then he raced to the front of The Impossible Dreams. He heard some of the Death Strides yelling for the black cloud to come back, they had a present for it.

Nick beat on the front door. Eventually Horatio unlocked it and Nick ran inside.

"Tom!"

Nick bumped into Fat Kid as Horatio unlocked the front door.

"Where's Tom?" Nick shouted.

"Well, he's right…" Horatio said as he turned back to where Tom was standing just a minute ago but the old man was gone.

Chapter Eight

It hadn't changed at all in the decades since he last visited the cubicle style plane. The smell of burning electrical wiring and the giggles from The Party Club door doors down were also present here. This was 91 Greene, his plane. It had been a home away from home when he was a boy. Tom never questioned the logic of his dreams when he was child. Why 91 Greene? Why were the demented leather-clad demons known as The Party Club just two doors down, laughing, and drinking, and having a party? Tom wasn't concerned about the logic of this realm or why it hadn't changed in almost one hundred years. What he was interested in was where had he hidden the footlocker. He knew this was the safest place. It wasn't until he put the pieces together that he realized that *he* was the one who had stolen the footlocker and hidden it away in the one place he knew was safe, his own mind. When he saw the Borden Hatchet missing his subconscious had kicked in.

"Bingo!"

Tom raced down the narrow corridor and knocked on Barlow's door. Barlow, being the green-headed mallard in the brown rumpled corduroy suit. He hadn't seen the Pooka in forever and began to sweat feeling the anxiety of time strike him now. Removing the old Fedora, Tom wiped a layer of sweat from his lined forehead and knocked again.

After several seconds he knocked a third time. On the third knock the cubicle apartment door creaked open.

"Barlow," Tom whispered, hearing how strange the name sounded coming from his old vocal cords.

Pushing open the small green metal door Tom stepped through ducking his head. He hadn't had to do that as a child, but now he was several feet taller. The entire apartment really did resemble a cubicle in a very cramped way. As a boy Tom thought of this place as cozy and safe. Barlow was always there for him. They had traveled the high seas together and tripped into outer space through Tom's childhood imagination. Barlow had been a facilitator for this imagination. He told Tom that he was a special boy who could create things. Those adventures that he and Barlow took were the boy's pure imagination.

Looking around the remains of Barlow's strange cubicle Tom started to remember more about his childhood and about the owners of The Impossible Dreams, the Logos. The Logos were the cosmic creators of great Poles of Existence. They wore corduroy jackets and…that's when Tom saw the old miniature corduroy suit lying on the floor next to the closet. It was Barlow's suit, the brown one that he wore on all of their adventures.

"Barlow?" Tom called out and as quick as he called out he heard the laughter two doors down. It was the horrible Party Club.

Tom looked to the front door where he heard the demented Party Club, laughing and drinking and having a party. Had they taken Barlow? Had they eaten him? He was a duck after all, or that's the form he took in Tom's mind.

Looking back around the cubicle apartment he remembered why he had come and where he had hidden the footlocker.

"Psyche Tree," he whispered.

#

"Where is he? Where is that *rat*!" Dogg bellowed into the store as he pushed his way through the front entrance. He was looking for old Tom and he was angry and with good reason. Mel, one of his best friends and world class mechanic was gone, stolen by the evil that Tom had unleashed on the world.

His large hands were bleeding from digging on the pavement out front searching for Mel. Dogg knew she was gone, sucked up by that black ectoplasmic cloud. The Death Strides entered the small front of the store too looking for old Tom.

"Where'd he go?" Patty asked.

Barb's leather gloved hands were on her hips.

"What a bust. Come on girls, maybe we can still make the Pete's slaughterhouse gig," Barb snarled as she turned to leave.

"Wait!" It was Horatio running to the front of the store to try and stop the women.

Barb, Tammy, and Patty all hesitated and looked back at Fat Kid.

"Wait? Wait for what? This is just jerkin' time," Patty said.

"You're just going to give up?"

Horatio looked at all of them, The Death Strides, Nick, the Bokar Brothers, and Dogg. Fish wasn't present, neither was Rachel.

"I'm not giving up. First I'm gonna kill that old fart then Dogg's gonna hunt down this darkness and *kill* it!"

"Where's Fish," Nick asked.

"Who gives a rat's tukus about that loser? He ain't done nuthin' but bring you down boy," Dogg said.

Nick just looked at Dogg with disgust for a second and then sprinted out the door.

"Nick!"

Horatio watched his new friend disappear out the door. Fat Kid looked at the Bokar Brothers who were just standing there stunned not speaking. This was a first for Charlie Bokar.

"Come on Chuck, Hank, let's find Rachel," Horatio said.

"Boy, you nuts? You go out there with nothin' ta protect yerself that darkness will eat you alive."

Dogg was standing with his hands on his hips. Everyone was watching this exchange.

"You're so selfish, and believe me I know about selfish. My mother…I mean, I'm sorry you lost your friend, Mel. But is she really gone? And what's it solve getting down on Nick because his best friend's a slacker? BIG DEAL! We're looking at the death of everyone here. We need to work together to stop this evil or we're all toast," Horatio said.

What followed this spiel was a long uncomfortable silence and then Barb clapped her leather gloved hands together.

"Well spoken, kid. Your dad a politician?"

"Nah, he's a logger," Dogg said grinning. "Okay yer right, kid. Let's move."

Henry and Charlie raced for the door pushing one another aside. Patty swatted them as she walked by. Charlie blushed. They were all exiting the store when the basement door slammed open. Horatio stopped and turned back.

"Tom!"

He ran to the old man who emerged from the door holding the footlocker.

"Holy cow! Tom found the footlocker," Charlie said running back toward the old proprietor.

"Tom, man, you look horrible!"

Henry was reaching out to help Tom because the old man looked like he was about to faint. He was corpse pale and his gray hair was white now.

His old Fedora was missing. It looked strange to see Tom without it on his wooly head.

"Tom? Tom, are you okay?"

Horatio helped Henry set Tom down on a nearby stool. Charlie was already riffling through the footlocker searching for his werewolf mask.

"Where is it? Where's the..." Charlie was totally panicked but then they all saw him pull the scruffy tangled mess of his werewolf mask from the wooden footlocker.

"Cool," Henry said reaching in for his old Civil War zombie jacket and cap.

"Come on Horatio, grab your suit," Charlie said as he was about to slide on the mask.

Fat Kid was looking at Tom. The old man looked like he had aged about fifty years.

"Fat Kid, come on. We got stuff to do," Charlie said.

Barb and the Death Strides stepped forward to see the old footlocker.

"Look at it girls. Can you believe it?" Barb said motioning toward the ancient footlocker with its archaic symbols etched into the wood.

162

"Wow, haven't seen that bad boy in a coon's age," Patty said.

Even Dogg stepped forward in reverence removing his old baseball cap.

"I'll be," he smiled, a tear fell on his scruffy pitted cheek.

They all watched as Dogg stepped forward placing his baseball cap along his chest as if mourning someone once loved and lost. He brushed at his tired wet eyes and then reached out for the footlocker. At first Charlie didn't seem to want to let it go but Horatio took it from the boy and handed it over to Dogg who just grinned like an old fool.

"See...this here footlocker, this saved my life," Dogg said.

His bright eyes looked at the others.

"Y'all wanta know why Dogg hates old Tom? 'Cause what comes out of this footlocker might have saved *my* life but it killed my brother, Coffey."

The entire store was silent for a long time. When someone finally did speak it was old Tom.

"Dogg, that footlocker never killed Coffey. Coffey ain't dead."

Dogg glared at the old man as if he was telling the worst fart joke on the books.

"Yer kiddin'? Coffey been gone fer years. I ain't heard a peep and we was thick as thieves. But yer tellin' me my brother is still alive. Why not tell me this before?"

Tom shrugged.

"You stopped takin' my calls."

"Why you old coot," Dogg said rushing forward but The Death Strides interceded.

Barb and the girls blocked Tom with their arms crossed over their breasts. No one messed with the Death Strides, Dogg knew it. As big as he was, and he towered over the three women, he still stepped back.

"What about Mel? She's dead and that's on you."

Dogg slid on his baseball cap and stormed out of the store.

The Bokar Brothers were holding their costumes waiting for Horatio perhaps. Fat Kid knelt down and snatched his super hero suit from the interior of the footlocker that Dogg had dropped on his way out of the store.

A second later he was standing over six feet tall with a chest the size of a mac truck. The Death Strides all grinned at his immensity. Charlie and Henry also transformed into the werewolf and Civil War zombie.

"P-U," Tammy said as she stood next to Henry's undead corpse.

She removed a small perfume spritzer and dowsed Henry with it. He coughed up a lung, literally, and when he handed it to her she glared at him. That done, he swallowed the lung repositioning it in his rib cage and then he followed his brother out of the store.

"Tom, where did you find the footlocker?" Fat Kid asked.

"That's a longer story than we have time to tell now. Maybe once this evil is all sealed up I'll tell ya. But now you gotta git out there and save the world. It's what you were born to do boy," Tom said.

He was staring up at the super hero Horatio. Fat Kid stood about two feet taller than anyone else around him. He was itching to find Rachel. He knew that she was out there somewhere searching for that monkey, which wasn't *really* a monkey after all.

"Stay safe Tom. We'll be back."

Fat Kid's voice boomed inside the store and he flew out through the open door.

"Nice," Barb said grinning as she and the Death Strides headed for the door.

"Barb?"

Barb turned back when she heard Tom's voice.

"Take care of them. Please," the tears in the old man's voice were undeniable.

Barb nodded snapping her gum as the girls exited the store. Tom rushed to the front door and locked it.

#

Where was he going? Fish had seen some messed up ghosts in his time but that black ecto cloud thingy was the worst. It joggled his mind. Every muscle and cell of his body felt warped. He had been possessed by that black cloud. Fish had seen its collective consciousness. He saw something lurking beneath the folds of the blackness, something that pulsed with utter destruction.

It was a man, or resembled a man, lean almost nondescript except for the eyes, which were pure blackness like the ecto cloud itself.

Fish withered then dropping to the sidewalk beneath a flickering street light. It felt like the world was coming to an end. For Fish it was. He had seen man's destruction in the embodiment of this stranger that walked in darkness with black eyes like bottomless pools with horrible creatures swimming within. The only designation for this stranger that Fish could find in his memory was – The GERMAN.

He broke down bawling like a small child deserted on the street. Boogey monsters did exist. They killed kids with hatchets, stole them into dark realms and did unspeakable experiments on them. Small children, small girls, small girls...

Fish glanced up feeling the presence of something next to him and he saw two small girls with blackened facial features. A second later the flickering street light went out and he sat on the sidewalk in darkness as the two little girls morphed into the ecto cloud.

"Fish," he heard Nick's voice somewhere down the block.

It was too late though. The darkness was surrounding him scooping him up like a giant cosmic vacuum cleaner. One second Fish was crying on the sidewalk and the next he was gone.

#

When Dogg reached Nick the young guy was on his knees crying for his best friend. Fish was nowhere to be seen and neither was the darkness that Dogg knew must have been here to cause Nick to end up in such a miserable state.

"Son, Nick, where's Fish?"

"Gone…he's gone, Dogg!"

Nick screamed. He had lost it, finally the controlled always prepared Nick, was crumbling. Dogg dropped to a single knee and embraced the skinny guy.

"Hey, hey it's okay we'll find him."

"How? How can we find him? He's gone. I stood right over there and watched as two little girls turned into the black ectoplasm. It snatched him from our reality Dogg. He could be anywhere, or *nowhere*?"

Dogg gave this a thought as the werewolf, zombie, and super hero came around the corner. He was startled by their presence at first but quickly recovered when he rationalized that Tom's footlocker had to be involved.

"Horatio?" Dogg asked when the tall massive super hero dropped down next to him.

"Yes it's me. Did you find Fish?"

Dogg's broken features and Nick's red eyes pretty much said it all. Fish was gone.

Horatio lifted into the air and glanced up and down the streets but saw nothing.

"What happened?" Henry slurred through his undead lips. Many of his broken and crooked teeth were missing. His purple tongue dangled from his mouth like a dead eel.

"The darkness took him, just sucked him up," Nick said.

"Like Mel," Dogg said.

"We need to track that cloud, find its origins," Charlie snarled through his long fanged muzzle.

"But how? It's gone?" Nick said.

"We got it covered."

They all turned to see the three Death Strides standing next to their cool van. The back doors were wide open. The small group, Fat Kid, Henry, Charlie, Nick, and Dogg stepped up to the back of the van where Tammy was typing feverishly on a keyboard. Barb had strapped on her silver Sterling ghost buster guitar. Patty was carrying her bass and grinned at the monsters as they lumbered forward.

"Tom got you dudes too, I see," Patty smirked.

Henry grinned as a long spool of drool ran over his lower lip. Charlie howled into the night sky laughing like a crazy hyena. Patty's grin widened and she strummed on her electric bass. The notes rang through the night like tightening electrical cords. They all felt the power surge and the street light above the sidewalk flickered back on.

Charlie covered his ears and howled. The bass was like a dog whistle for him and he cried out, snarling at her. Patty just grinned again at the wild werewolf.

"Mind tellin' us what you girls got?"

Dogg had relit his cigar and blew out some smoke.

"Stow those cigar toxins. We're all natural here, *Dogg*," Barb said kicking the cigar from Dogg's grimy lips.

The black man stepped back, shocked at Barb's speed.

The cigar rolled across the sidewalk into the gutter and then whiffed out.

"Been working out?"

"Always," Barb nodded.

"Anyway," Tammy said motioning for everyone to take a look at her monitor.

They all came in to view what Tammy wanted to show them.

"Okay, what you're looking at is a digital tracking of the molecular elements of the black ectoplasmic cloud," Tammy said.

Henry and Charlie just looked at one another in a mystified shrug. Nick thought that if Fish was here he would ask for the Cliff Notes version. This made him feel even more miserable.

"The cloud is made up of a molecular structure that we rarely have seen, but we *have* seen it. I think we can seriously capture it but…"

They all waited for the answer to that "but".

"Based off the size of the cloud and its ability to appear and disappear at will, trapping something like this will require a serious carrot."

"Carrot?" Henry drooled.

"Yeah, to draw it out. Once it's out in the open and we can kick in our Big'en, the lights go out, we trap it in our storage facility and then start working on a way to actually destroy it. Sound like a plan?"

Tammy was real proud of herself.

"So what's a big enough carrot to draw it out?" Dogg asked. He was smoking on a new cigar now.

Everyone was silent for a minute and then a voice from the corner called to them.

"Me!"

All eyes switched to the corner. Tom stood there grinning.

#

Fat Kid was in the air now flying over the city streets looking for the darkness that had retreated back into the city shadows. He had lied to the others. Sort of anyway. Horatio wanted to help Fish but he really wanted to find Rachel. She had been gone for far too long. He had seen what the black cloud could do, not only with the deaths of the two kids, but also with the abduction of Mel right before their eyes. If Rachel had gone looking for the darkness she may have found it. What that meant, Horatio didn't want to think about.

When he saw the shining light far off in the sky Horatio thought maybe he was developing a new super hero talent. When he saw the fabric of reality slice open and Rachel Brooks flew out he wasn't sure to scream with joy or terror. Rachel didn't look like herself. She was of course dressed as the vampire queen but something else had changed about her appearance. The green pre-teen eyes that Horatio had fallen in love with were replaced by pools of blackness.

"Rachel?"

She turned to face him as he noticed how the split in the fabric of reality sealed up behind her. She was carrying a glowing hatchet. Immediately he felt drawn to the item reminding him of Golem with his *precious* ring. Horatio flew forward toward

173

Rachel. The closer he went the stronger the hatchet pulsed. It wanted him and he wanted it.

"Rachel, where did you get that?"

She looked at him, through him.

"You are not the boy. I seek the boy."

Fat Kid narrowed his brow as she flew past him. A second later he was flying next to her.

"Rachel what's wrong with you? What boy are you talking about?"

In response she swung the hatchet but Horatio was quick. He flew sideways well out of the hatchet's range. The glowing of the hatchet seemed to falter but then recharged. It glowed in the night sky like a supernova then.

"Rachel?"

The super hero voice commanded her to stop. Rachel hesitated in the sky levitating, staring at Fat Kid in his super hero suit.

"Stay out of my way, or you will die."

In response to this Horatio actually flew into her path with his massive muscled arms crossed over his equally massive chest.

"Rachel, you are not yourself. I see it in your eyes. That hatchet has bled children…"

"And so much more," Rachel said and launched herself like a bullet at him.

The meat of the hatchet's flat surface struck Horatio and he flew backwards doing somersaults in the air. He continued head over heels, over and over again. The place of contact on his chest where the hatchet struck burned like hot coals.

His mind whirled like a ship on a raging ocean. Horatio couldn't stop flipping and he felt a black chaos rush up to him beating him about the head. His father's voice surfaced among the chaos, but unlike the usual supportiveness, his father was yelling at him trying to tear him down. This was the final emotional nail in his coffin. As much as Horatio wanted to fight, hearing his father scream at him, having seen Rachel transformed into the evil creature that had struck him, he couldn't fight as the darkness enclosed around him and he vanished.

#

"You? How do you figure into this?" Barb said.

"Shoulda know'd you have somethin' to do with this. Finally takin' the high road and payin' fer yo sins?" Dogg asked glaring at old Tom.

"Something like that," Tom said.

He spent the next several minutes trying as quickly as he could to explain why he believed the darkness was looking for him.

"So you think that this evil wants you because you can, what, create stuff?" Nick asked not quite getting Tom's pitch.

"See, when I was a small boy I travelled, up here," Tom said pointing to his head. "There was always a place I went to, 91 Greene, another Pole you might call it. Barlow..."

"That's your Pooka?" Tammy asked.

"Yeah, Barlow my Pooka and I went on all kinds of adventures, but he always said it was *me* who could do the creating. Said I was special."

"How sweet," Dogg said scorning.

"Shhh!" Henry and Charlie both said as Henry lost another tooth.

Dogg just frowned puffing off his cigar.

"Now not to get too much into my history let me just say there was a reason those cosmic fellas who created all of this gave me the keys to the Impossible Dreams," Tom said.

"Impossible Dreams? That name's making more and more sense now," Patty said.

They all nodded.

"See, them fellas that created our world, I heard them called the Logos, they gave old Tom the keys to the kingdom so to speak…"

"Keys to the kingdom? Why does that sound familiar?" Nick asked.

"Because there is such a place, The Keys To The Kingdom. It's a horrible place filled with all kinds of dark spirits, entities you call them…"

"Off the charts, and you done opened this portal up to Earth and now we're all getting sucked down the drain," Dogg spit on the ground next to Tom's feet.

"I'm here now you damned Dogg and I'm planning to make amends. Old Tom's not hidin' no more," Tom shouted at them.

Dogg snorted his disapproval. Tammy and Nick reached out and hugged old Tom.

"Okay enough of this Mickey Mouse stroll down memory lane, better get a move on. That darkness is spreading and there's no telling how fast it's moving," Barb said,

"Or where it is now." Patty said.

"I have an answer for that."

Tammy let Tom go and ran back to the van. She keyed in a few strokes on the computer. A large red dot appeared on the screen with a digital map. Pointing at the red dot Tammy turned back to the group smiling.

"That's it. That's the bulk of the cloud."

"Well that's convenient," Dogg said looking at the red dot move and shift on the map. "What's the coordinates?"

Tammy typed in some more key strokes.

"Should be…right about there," she said pointing just outside of the van.

A second later the world became black and they were all dowsed in the floating ectoplasmic cloud. Charlie's werewolf howling and Henry's zombie screams could be heard but no one could see anything.

Nick slid on his headphones and switched on The Hose. The first thing he heard was the dark voices of little girls whispering unintelligibly, or maybe it was another language. With the headphones on the chaos of screams and panic ceased outside. Now it was Nick, the darkness and the childish whispers. He adjusted the volume on his belt and he could hear the whispers.

The child. We have the child.

"Tom," Nick said but could only hear it in his head.

A second later the black cloud was gone. They were all covered in a gooey ectoplasm. Nick saw the small band shouting and complaining about the mess but the world remained silent inside his headphones. Looking around he saw, the werewolf, the zombie, the three Death Strides, and Dogg.

"Tom," he said dropping his headphones.

They all stopped shouting and looked at Nick.

"Tom's gone."

"Good riddance. Now maybe that evil will stay where it belongs," Dogg said spitting black goo onto the sidewalk.

"You're a jerk," Tammy said.

"And a bully," Barb echoed her sister in arms.

Dogg just looked them over and strutted off.

"Wait Dogg, we need to stick together," Nick said.

"Let him go," Barb said she was speed dialing someone on her cell phone.

"Who you calling?" Patty asked.

"Corporate," Barb said.

Patty and Tammy went silent. Henry and Charlie both noticed the uncomfortable feeling and turned to Nick.

"Nick, what's with the sisters?" Charlie snarled.

"Yeah, who's corporate?" Henry slurred.

Nick looked at the two monsters before him. He was constantly amazed by the magic of Impossible Dreams. He was brushing off the black ecto goo when he started to tell them about the Dream Police.

"The Dream Police are the elite of ghost hunters in DenMark. They cover all corporate gigs. They own a skyscraper on Park Ave," Nick said watching Barb speak with someone from the Dream Police.

After another minute Barb ended the call.

"Let's load up. George will take us a-sap!"

She snapped her leather fingers. Tammy and Patty loaded back into their van while Nick led the werewolf and zombie back to Flo, the VW van. Henry pushed Charlie and Charlie pushed him back, wrestling for the shotgun seat. It was quite comical to see a werewolf and a zombie pushing each other to get the front seat of the old VW van. Nick might have laughed if they weren't in such dire straits.

Chapter Nine

They sat as silent as if they were in church. Charlie and Henry had only been in church once when their Aunt Carol had taken them against their will. She thought maybe she would put the fear of God into them, she was wrong. The Bokar Brothers would never be angels. Henry looked at his brother Charlie fully transformed into a werewolf and giggled.

Looking at the size of the lobby with its vaulted ceilings Henry felt like he was in church. This Dream Police corporation was so clean and angelic feeling that Henry felt dirty just sitting in their lobby. Charlie had fallen asleep about twenty minutes ago as they all sat waiting for the corporate bigwig to take them in. When the receptionist got the call for them to go inside Henry had been fighting sleep as well.

"He'll see you now," the receptionist said.

As the small group walked past the receptionist Henry was surprised that she didn't look twice at he and Charlie, Henry being a zombie and Charlie a werewolf. Henry guessed that that chick had seen stranger things wander through the lobby than a werewolf and zombie.

"We're off to see the wizard," Charlie said as they entered the office. He was yawning and stretching.

Barb took the lead once they were inside the CEO's office.

As they entered the group noticed there wasn't a lick of furniture except a wide metal table and a high back chair on the other side. The chair's back was to them and they saw only the top of a head. The sounds of a mumbled conversation came to them over the top of the chair. Henry glanced at Barb who stood glaring at the back of the chair. Her arms were crossed with her leather gloves and she was chewing her gum aggressively. Whoever the dude was that made them wait was going to get an earful. Henry stood back grinning until his eyes dropped to the name plate on the top of the desk – GEORGE BOKAR.

"What? Chuck, take a look," Henry said motioning to the name plate.

Charlie yawned his scraggy jaws and looked at the name plate. His eyes went wild.

"Bokar?"

Henry nodded as the chair swiveled around to face the small group. The initial image of the guy in the chair was less than impressive. His features were so conventional as to be boring except his chin. His chin spoke volumes with its pointy yet potato faced features. His hair was thick and black with hints of gray slicked straight back from his smooth flawless forehead. He looked to be mid to late forties. Henry noticed that the guy was wearing a tag on his lapel. The logo on the tag was the same as the image on the outside of the building, a skull wearing a police helmet with two sabers crossing behind the head. The image was cool, Henry had to admit it, and kind of out of place for such a stuffy corporation.

"George," Barb said.

"Barb, Patty, Tammy. And who are these creatures," George Bokar asked looking at the werewolf and zombie.

"Henry and Charlie *Bokar* sir," Henry and Charlie both rushed forward elbowing the other out of the way.

George smiled down at them from aloft his leather chair.

"Bokar? No relation," he said and then turned back to the Death Strides. "Got your call. It's just too bad we lost so many in the meantime."

Barb and the girls looked at each other.

"What are you talking about," Patty said.

"A one Horatio Patterson, Melvina Wachowski, Fish and poor old Tom," George said whistling his disappointment at their actions.

"Melvina…what?" Charlie asked.

"Mel, is Dogg's mechanic," Nick said stepping forward. He had been silent until now.

"Nicholas," George said nodding.

That look gave them all a hint at George Bokar and Nick's past association. They both appeared frosty toward the other.

"Fish and the others are not casualties of war, George. We can still pull them back."

"Oh Nick, always the optimist. Do you have any idea how many variables come into play once a being is sucked into the kind of ectoplasmic substance that has been spilling out of those cracks Tom opened for years? It's worse than the BP spill."

George pushed himself away from the desk and they all saw how tall and lean he was, practically presidential. This was the kind of guy who was always going places in life. Right then George glanced out the large wall sized window of his office and overlooked the dark city streets of DenMark.

"There has to be a way. Tammy?" Nick said turning to Tammy.

"I believe that we have found a way to track the black ectoplasm..."

"We're already doing that," George cut her off. "Don't you think a corporation like the Dream Police have covered all of our bases?"

"*Legally* maybe, but we're talking nuts and bolts here George," Barb said. She was finished being patient with this corporate hack.

"What would a piece of white trash like you know about nuts and bolts Barbie? Your females are nothing more than raving lunatics with hair. The Clock Strikes Ten aren't held together with more than a roll of Duct tape, and old worn out Duct tape at that," George said.

"Why you corporate hack," Barb said as she launched herself at him.

She threw a left punch, he dodged it easily. The right came quick but George sidestepped it and kicked her feet out from under her. Patty was already in motion removing a retractable steel wand from her belt. The wand opened but George had her on the desk disabled before she knew what happened. The end of the wand was pressed against Patty's throat. Tammy screamed but stood her ground. Barb went after George again with a series of kicks, roundhouse and front kicks. The front kick caught George in the chest and he lifted off his feet but caught himself on his hands and pushed back onto his feet in a fighting stance.

"Stop this!" Nick shouted as Henry and Charlie were about to enter the fight.

Charlie wailed a blood curdling howl inside the office. A second later there were several dark suited men who resembled ninjas standing in the open door. They held weapons that looked like industrial strength Tasers.

"This isn't helping and we're wasting time," Nick said.

"You wasted time the minute you signed up with that old stooge Tom. Your lives ever since have been nothing but a waste. Tell me I'm wrong?"

George looked at the sweaty Death Strides, Nick, and then at Henry and Charlie.

"Kids, I suggest you exit this office and never speak with Tom ever again. Words of advice from someone who knows. Now…" George straightened his tie as he sat back down at his desk without a single hair out of place. "Actions are being taken to secure the cracks created by Tom. If you believe that your friends are still alive I suggest you find them, because at dawn those cracks will be sealed forever."

#

Rachel, or the darkness that now possessed Rachel Brooks, saw the glowing tower of the Dream Police in the distance. The skyscraper was the brightest sight in the city. The hatchet she held was pulling her to this pulsing landmark. As she approached it she saw the large circular logo with the skull and police helmet with the sabers plunged in behind it.

#

"Would you gentlemen mind seeing our guests to the door?" George motioned for his dark suited ninjas to escort the small group out.

188

They started grabbing each of the guests and dragging them toward the door of the office when the large picture window imploded throwing shards of glass across the room. Screams filled the space as the black ecto cloud, led by Rachel Brooks, quickly filled the room. Within seconds they were all hidden inside the blackness.

Nick heard a series of screams start loud from someone was standing next to him and then those screams began to fade, as if the owner was thrown out the tower window. This image of figures falling from the skyscraper terrified Nick and he dropped to the ground grabbing for anything that would keep him stable. He felt around in the inky blackness and grabbed a foot. He heard a wolf's howl and knew that he had found Charlie.

"Charlie is Henry with you?"

The werewolf just moaned like a beaten dog. Nick could feel the kid's werewolf tongue lick the side of his face.

"I'm here," Henry whispered through his decrepit corpse lips. "What happened?"

"Not sure. Be quiet and hold on tight to one another," he said and a second later he felt himself being ripped from the safety of the office and flying out the broken shards of the window into the night sky.

Nick screamed as he fell seeing the city streets rush up beneath him.

"I'm sorry Fish, sorry Dogg, sorry everyone."

The concrete sidewalk was inches away and he thought he felt his skull crash on it but instead his lunch swam up from his stomach and vomited all over the sidewalk. A second later he turned and looked behind him. Levitating there was Horatio Patterson dressed in his bright super hero suit. The super hero had caught Nick's ankle in his massive fist.

"Horatio you saved me," Nick said, but then he noticed that the super hero's eyes were nothing but vacant white orbs.

This wasn't Horatio inside the suit now.

"Oh no," Nick said as he was lifted off the ground into the air again.

He flew up screaming and then saw something fly at him like a lightning bolt. Whatever it was struck the evil Horatio and he dropped Nick. Nick fell over sixty flights feeling like he was a human bungee cord but this time the person who snatched his ankle was the real Horatio. Nick saw the super hero's eyes. Despite him being much larger and more muscular the kind eyes of Horatio Patterson were solidly inside the mask.

"Horatio is that you?"

"It's me," he said but then the evil Horatio flew past striking our hero across the square jaw. He dropped Nick again.

Inside the office George was taking immediate action. He slammed his fist down on a red button on his desk as a metal shield came down over the open window. A second later the sound of industrial vents boomed across the office as the black cloud cleared. When they could all see again most of the black suited ninja style Dream Police were gone – thrown out the window. Charlie and Henry were hugging one another. Barb was helping Tammy to her feet and Patty was wiping blood from her eyes. They were all dowsed with the gooey black ectoplasm.

"Where's Nick?" someone said.

All eyes shifted to the floating vampire in the room. George removed a long barreled weapon from his desk and sighted Rachel in the crosshairs.

"No!" Henry and Charlie both shouted.

"I'm not taking any chances," George shouted back as Rachel spun around and threw the hatchet at him. The steel blade embedded itself in the top of the metal table. He fired the pistol. A dart punctured Rachel's breast through the front of her gown startling her. A second later George had the hatchet wrapped in a strange fabric bag. A metal briefcase was slid onto the desk and the hatchet was slid inside and latched in safely.

Rachel hit the ground once the hatchet was securely placed in the metal briefcase as if someone had hit her power switch. The drug finally hit home. Henry and Charlie moved as fast as they could to Brooks's side. Charlie got there quicker on his werewolf legs. He lifted Rachel's head onto his furry knees as Henry approached looking down drooling.

"Brooks? Brooks, wake up! Oh man, where's Fat Kid when you need him?"

A second later a huge fist print plunged into the metal of the shield covering the busted window. Two more hits and they saw Horatio's face peer through the new hole he beat through the metal. George was on his feet carrying the case out of the office.

"Where's he going?" Barb asked.

Barb and the other Death Strides raced after George.

"Horatio! Rachel's hurt," Henry said.

Fat Kid shot both of his fists through the metal shield and then tore it off the side of the building. Flying inside he lifted Rachel off Charlie's furry knees. Fat Kid dropped Nick, who was cupped under one of his massive muscled arms, onto the expensive office carpet where Nick squirmed away from the shock of being a human bungee cord.

"What happened?"

"Brooks busted in carrying a hatchet. I think it was the Borden Hatchet Tom talked about," Henry said.

"That creep George stole it and left," Charlie snarled pointing toward the open office door. Charlie looked at Nick who was white as a sheet. "What happened to him?"

"My Doppelganger, came from 91 Greene, long story. I need to get that hatchet," he said and then dropped Rachel into Henry and Charlie's arms like a bag of oats.

"Fat Kid, what the heck?" Henry said.

"I can't explain right now but it's extremely important that I collect that hatchet."

Horatio flew from the office leaving Henry and Charlie to hold Rachel.

#

George Bokar made it to the door of his safe room. He started punching in the code to access the room when he saw Barb, Patty, and Tammy rounding the corner on a dead sprint. They meant business. George never fumbled with his digits and seconds later the door hissed open.

The Death Strides arrived nearly too late but Barb was quick. She flew in the air with a dragon death kick striking George in the back. Unfortunately for them, that was the momentum Bokar needed to make it through the door. It left him a few seconds before the Death Strides hit his safe room door.

Feeling the pain from Barb's kick pulse along his spine George was still able to get to his feet and reach out to hit the red lock button on the door.

"Don't touch that dial," Patty shouted through the crack in the door.

George grinned sardonically and slammed his hand into the button and the door shut. Tammy and Barb pulled Patty away just in time. With her adrenaline pumping she meant to slide through the crack in the closing door, which would have ended in her being sliced in half. That meant George Bokar was playing for blood. The Death Strides and the Dream Police never worked well together but at least they seemed to appreciate one another's drive. This ended that.

"Idiot!" Barb slammed her leather gloved hands against the steel of the door.

"He almost killed me," Patty said awed and then she was on her feet kicking savagely at the door with her steel-toed cowboy boots.

"Don't bother, that door has a carbon lock. Nothing's getting through that," Tammy said, but that's when Fat Kid flew past them with hell flashing through his eyes.

He struck the safe door knocking it off its massive hinges. The door shot across the room nearly strike George in the process. The first thing Fat Kid saw was this George Bokar character standing in front of what Horatio might think of as a portal. The portal was glowing and faded along the edges into the wall behind it. There was a man on the other side, at least he looked like a man, but every fiber of Horatio's being told him that what he was looking at in that portal was no man. There was something familiar about the man's face. He resembled one of Fat Kid's father's favorite actors, Stephen McHattie.

Horatio felt so bizarre standing there looking at his father's favorite actor. That's when he remembered being trapped inside the black cloud hearing his father's usual supportive voice scorning him. How had he made it out? Rachel had sliced open reality again and he exited the blackness like walking through a split carnival tent. From one reality to another.

Fat Kid shook these thoughts off and stared back at George who was now totally consumed with handing over the metal briefcase to this creature on the other side of the portal.

"George no!" Barb and the other Death Strides had made it into the safe room.

George turned to see them as the stranger's hand, the GERMAN's hand, reached through the portal and snatched the case with the Borden Hatchet. George glanced back through the portal and saw the GERMAN blink and the portal closed. They all saw a device attached to the wall but for a second none of them actually processed what that device was because it looked like a shower curtain rod with a red shower curtain hanging from it. The curtains were draped open but the portal was gone, replaced by a black patch of burned wall.

"You!"

Horatio looked at George Bokar who seemed to shrivel away now dropping to the floor bawling like a small child. They all stared down at this absurd image in surprise. For as long as the Death Strides knew the CEO of the Dream Police, George Bokar, he was powerful and elusive. The ladies had actually privately all enjoyed knowing that the Dream Police were active and helping to keep the city safe from the larger more powerful entities out there. Looking at this shriveled bawling figure before them struck a note of terror in all their heroic hearts.

"What have you done? You gave the hatchet to…"

"The one being that assured me he can close these cracks!" George interrupted Horatio.

They all glanced at George as he pushed himself off the ground and stared at the burned patch of his wall.

"The only…are you kidding? That *thing* that you just handed the hatchet over to was from the other side. Nothing ever good comes from the other side, you know that," Barb was shouting now.

"You don't have a clue sister. You think that your silly little band running all over the city playing gigs and slaying entities really matters? Damn sister, you are dumb," George said returning to his arrogant self.

Barb went after him but Horatio stepped between them this time. Barb didn't have a chance.

"I want to hear what he has to say," Horatio's voice boomed with his super suit. He turned back to George. "Speak."

George looked at the Death Strides and the super hero and then straightened his tie.

"It all started in Idaho, what feels like a million years ago. The story is too long to tell here, but I used to be part of a small unit back then – the King Cobras. At that time there was me, a dude named Coffey, a Scotsman Duncan Dougal, and Morgue. Morgue was the toughest of us. The guy wouldn't go down no matter how many slugs he took. We each had a special touch, mine…opening doorways."

"Like this," Horatio said touching the black spot on the wall.

"Exactly, but this was so long ago and we're all separated now."

"Hey, didn't Dogg say something about Tom killing off his brother, Coffey?" Barb said to the others.

"Yeah, that's right he did," Patty said.

"But Tom said Coffey wasn't dead, whatever that meant," Tammy said.

"What it sounds like is old Tom's correct. Coffey is probably off somewhere in another Pole."

"Pole?" Horatio asked.

"It's what the Logos call their worlds. And before you ask don't ask about the Logos. That's an even longer story. Our unit helped these Logos keep the balance of reality in check. Old Tom was special because unlike the rest of us he had one greasy toe dipped in the creation biz. Like the Logos, Tom was a small scale creator. I guess that's why they gave him that run down old junk shop on Cobb Street."

"I'd say that The Impossible Dreams is a bit more than a rundown old junk shop," Horatio said flexing his massive biceps.

George just shrugged.

"Anyway, our little unit was what you might consider Special Op's. This went way back. There was a time called The War of Time Out of Mind when those dark beings on the other side meant to cross the fence, so to speak. The Logos employed us to help fix the cracks. Old Tom reopened them, poor schmuck. Now things have changed. Our unit is split like you all. Once this city had the opportunity to work together; different factions of ghost hunters now broken apart by their egos."

George just shook his self-righteous head.

"So how do we stop the black cloud from coming over?" Horatio asked.

"It's done. That little exchange you just witnessed essentially closed the gap," George said.

"What about our friends who are still over on the other side?" It was Nick now. He looked horrible standing in the open door with his pale complexion and wild hair.

"They're gone," George said.

He didn't seem too broken up about this, but for the others, like Nick who lost his best friend Fish, this was horrendous. Dogg would be feeling the same way having lost Mel to the darkness. Tom was also gone.

"This can't be. It can't be," Horatio repeated.

"It is kid. You can wear that suit as long as you want but at the end of the day you're just a kid in a costume."

The finality of George's words really hit home. Nick stood there stunned. It was like finding out that all of your dreams were nothing but a wash. Fat Kid looked at the Death Strides and then he exited the safe room. He reached down and lifted Rachel into his arms and started out of the office.

"Fat Kid wait," Henry said stumbling after him.

Charlie was on their heels as they left the office passing the receptionist who was speaking to someone on the phone. They left the Dream Police building without a word – destination: The Impossible Dreams.

Chapter Ten

The little blonde boy walked down the corridor for 91 Greene. He knew now that Barlow, like all Impossible Dreams, was an illusion. The stink of electrical wire and the insane giggles of The Party Club, two doors down laughing and drinking and having a party, filled his existence. Why hadn't this place changed in all of the years that he had been gone? He looked down at the young Tom's hands, Tom's feet, and Tom's face. The boy peered into a crooked tin can that reflected his childish image.

Tom, the boy, walked into the cubicle apartment where he visited Barlow, the green headed mallard, night after night.

The place felt empty again. He was here recently in a dream.

"The suit?"

Tom saw Barlow's brown rumpled corduroy suit and instead of crying over his lost friend, the lost friend's voice echoed in his mind – 'You're the one boy. You are *special*.'

"I wonder," Tom whispered.

A couple of minutes later he was wearing Barlow's old corduroy suit. It fit him perfect. When he glanced back at the dented can he saw his reflection and smiled.

#

They were all lost, especially Fish and Mel. For some reason when Fish opened his eyes on the other side after the black cloud took him he was sitting next to a brick wall and Mel was sitting some distance away. Her back was to him and she was still dressed in her greasy coveralls. Mel was working on something at a desk under a twisted wire table lamp.

"Mel?"

She swiveled around on her leather chair. She was wearing headphones and now Fish saw what she was tinkering with. He wasn't exactly sure what it was just that it looked like an old shortwave radio system.

"Fish?"

Fish pushed himself up off the hard floor. Vertigo slammed into him and Fish held the brick wall for a second until his mind stopped spinning. He smelled the burnt electrical wiring. Opening his eyes he blinked away the smoke.

"Where the heck are we?"

Fish waited until he was stable and then pushed himself forward toward her.

"We're somewhere among the Poles," Mel said.

"Poles?"

"Yeah, it's something Dogg mentioned on one of his drunken toots. He said something about the gods, or the Logos, and...well, based off his crazy drunken speech this place looks like what he was talking about," Mel said.

"Poles..."

Fish shook his head and walked around the small square cubicle they found themselves in. Mel had gone back to messing with the shortwave radio thing. He stood over Mel's shoulder. Fish towered over her. Mel was short and pretty and Fish always thought that under better circumstances he might find her kinda cute.

"What are you working on there?"

"It's some kind of a shortwave radio system. I found a whole binder with what looks like other sites," Mel said motioning to a dusty old black binder.

"Other sites?"

Fish lifted the binder and opened to the first page. In large print on the front page it read: Cellar Dweller directory.

"Cellar Dweller?"

"Yeah, it seems that the binder is a directory for all kinds of other locations. I assume since they are titled, Cellar Dwellers, they live underground, which is where we probably are now."

When the radio on the desk squawked to life Fish and Mel both jumped grabbing each other. A second later they looked into each other's eyes and then let go blushing. Fish fingered his goatee nervously.

"Hello?"

A voice broke through the line of static.

"Hello?"

It repeated.

Mel sat on the leather rolling chair and pushed herself forward putting the headphones on and she pressed the TALK button.

"Hello, who's there?" Mel said into the microphone.

"Who is this? What's your site number?"

Mel snapped her fingers and motioned for Fish to give her the black binder. He did and she riffled through the pages and found the page with a number aggressively circled.

"Operator 42, 42 we are at site 42," she said.

There was a long silence as Mel was sweating and Fish stared at the speakers nervously.

"That's a lost site. How did you get there?"

"We're not sure," Mel said.

"*We*?"

"Fish and me. I'm Mel. We were scooped up by some black ectoplasmic cloud and we woke up here."

Another long pause followed this. The pause was so long this time that Mel was convinced that the other speaker had dropped off.

"Stay tuned in. We'll be in touch."

Then the line went dead and Mel and Fish just sat there waiting.

#

Horatio and the Bokar Brothers arrived back at The Impossible Dreams sometime after the events in the Dream Police head office. The store was still unlocked. Once inside Henry locked the door and dropped the blinds.

Fat Kid brought Rachel to an old dusty sofa. The sofa was piled with a bunch of boxes but Fat Kid made fast work of that, and then laid Rachel down kissing her forehead. Was she alive, or dead? He wasn't sure about that because of the ice cold vampire persona, but he was positive that those Hatchet Sisters and the dark ecto cloud were going to pay for what they had done.

Henry and Charlie stood next to Fat Kid looking down at Rachel who was still unconscious due to George Bokar's dart that he shot into her.

"I need you guys to stay with Rachel. I have some things to take care of," Horatio said.

"Wait a minute. We're not gonna just sit around here playing doctor while you go off and play hero," Henry said.

"I wouldn't mind playing doctor with Brooks," Charlie said glaring down through his werewolf eyes.

Henry elbowed his brother and Charlie elbowed him back.

"Just stay put. What I have to do is personal."

With that Horatio flew from the store like a speeding bullet leaving the Bokar Brothers to just stare down at Rachel Brooks.

"You know, she kinda looks like one of them vampires that hibernate in their coffins in them old Hammer flicks," Charlie said.

"Yeah," Henry said slumping on the floor next to the sofa feeling a little more than creeped out.

#

The Death Strides were cruising down the Southside of the city in their hopped up van when they received a transmission on their C.B. radio.

"Hello?"

A voice broke through the line of static.

"Hello?"

It repeated. The girls looked at each other.

"Who the heck is that?" Barb asked tuning in the transmission.

"Not sure. What station we on?"

Patty was driving and smoking a cigarette. She glanced down at the radio as Barb continued tuning in the transmission.

"Hello, who's there?" A familiar female voice echoed across the radio.

Barb finally got the transmission tuned in clear.

"Who is this? What's your site number?" A second male voice piped in.

Tammy sat forward in the back seat.

"What is this, one of those old time radio shows?" Tammy asked.

"Shhh! Listen," Barb said.

They all leaned forward.

"Operator 42, 42 we are at site 42," the female voice said.

There was a long silence. Barb looked at the others.

"That sounds like Mel, Dogg's mechanic."

The others nodded their agreement.

"That's a lost site. How did you get there?" The male voice came across the line again.

"We're not sure," Mel said.

"*We?*"

"Fish and me. I'm Mel. We were scooped up by some black ectoplasmic cloud and we woke up here."

Tammy leaned real close to the others now. They were all listening intently.

"It is Mel," Tammy said.

"And Fish," Patty said.

They all listened to the silence for another minute and the male voice came back across the line.

"Stay tuned in. We'll be in touch."

That's when the transmission went dead. Barb reached out and snagged the mic to the C.B. and hit the TALK button.

"Hello, hello is anyone out there?"

"Yeah sure honey, where you at? I could use some company tonight," an old gnarly sounding trucker's voice came across the line.

210

"Get off this line idiot we're trying to speak with someone important. It's an emergency," Barb snarled into the mic.

"Oh," the trucker dropped off.

The Death Strides just shook their heads – *idiots*.

"Hello," Mel's voice whispered.

"Mel is that you?"

"Who's this?"

"Barb Bigby from the Death Strides. Where the heck are you and Fish?"

"Barb, oh my god. We're in someplace with the operating number 42."

"Operating number? What the heck's that mean?"

"Long story. Anyway we're waiting to hear back from that other Cellar Dweller," Mel said.

"Cellar Dweller?"

"Even longer story. Is everyone else okay?"

"Rachel, the Bokar Brothers, and Horatio are back at Impossible Dreams, Tom's still missing and Dogg went after you guys. Have you seen him?"

"Dogg's looking for us? Really?"

"Yeah after George, the moron, Bokar gave the Borden Hatchet to that creepy GERMAN guy..."

"Wait! What? Creepy GERMAN guy?"

"Long story. Anyway, I think Nick's still at the Dream Police offices. George is probably trying to recruit him but Nick'll never sign with that jerk," Barb said and the others both nodded.

"Why?"

"Because he essentially sealed your..." Barb cut off for a second and looked at her sisters in arms. "Shoot."

"Barb, are you still there? What did you say about sealing *our*... What?"

"I was just saying that Nick wasn't happy about the deal with the GERMAN."

Barb blushed with anger and frustration.

"Can you guys stay on the line with us? It's kinda spooky here."

"Sure, we're here. If you can give us any clue to where you are that would help," Barb sat back.

Then Tammy snapped her fingers and slid back into the central computer area of the van. Patty and Barb just looked at one another and shrugged.

Tammy slid into her swivel chair that had been bolted to the van's base to keep it stable while Patty sped through the city. There had been plenty of nights racing through the city streets to some gig or ghost sighting when Tammy had been bruised way too many times not to have a bolted chair.

Tammy switched on her computer and the entity database that she had stored.

"Tam, what are you doing?" Patty asked watching her sister in the rearview mirror.

"I have a theory and if my theory is correct we might be able to triangulate where Mel's transmission is coming from and that can help us..."

"Find them. Excellent work Tam," Barb said.

She pressed the TALK button and spoke to Mel.

"Mel we might have some good news. Tam thinks she might be able to triangulate your transmission," Barb said.

Tammy continued to type away on her keyboard as The Death Strides' van sped through the city streets.

#

Fat Kid had had enough of this CEO corporate douche bag.

He flew to the head offices of the Dream Police Ghost Hunters on Park Avenue. When he arrived he noticed that the metal shield that had covered the front window had been replaced by a brand new piece of plate glass. Grinning Horatio launched himself through the plate glass window.

"*Man*," George Bokar said glaring at the super hero who levitated inside his office.

The shards of glass littered the office's expensive carpeting. Seconds after his explosive entrance the office was filled with black suited ninja style agents.

"It's all right," George said to his men but they did not exit the office.

214

Fat Kid just glared at them.

"Who is this GERMAN that you gave *my* hatchet to?"

George hesitated before answering, taken aback by the assumption that the Borden Hatchet was this pathetic kid's.

"What makes you think the hatchet is yours?"

"It's mine, trust me on that," Fat Kid said.

He felt a dangerous level of anger charging through his body now. He could snap this skinny guy in two.

"Trust you? A kid, how old are you anyway? Ten, eleven? Kid, you don't have a clue what lies outside those borders."

"Borders?"

"The walls of reality. People believe that they are safe living their puny little lives, watching television, playing with their little digital gadgets. The truth is there is so much evil out there sharpening its teeth to devour us. The human race, Earth, we're the last physical holdout for existence. That hatchet that you believe is *your* property was our best bargaining chip. That entity, ZEE

GERMAN, is beyond powerful. He could just poof you out of existence," George said adjusting his tie.

"But there has to be a way in. There has to be a way to at least save our friends."

"Your friends are not my concern," George said.

"What about Tom?"

"What about him. Do you know what that old bastard did? He opened old wounds that were once sealed by the Logos after the Great War. He went searching like a...like a *kid*," George said motioning to Fat Kid before him.

"So you're saying Mel, Fish, old Tom, they're just what, a sacrifice?"

"Collateral damage, kid. Now if you'll excuse me I have agents on the ground mopping up the rest of that black ectoplasm that seeped out."

George thought that he was through with the kid. He turned back to his computer and entered some key strokes as Fat Kid stood silently waiting. The black suited agents stood waiting for Horatio to leave.

Before even Fat Kid knew what he was doing he had snagged George Bokar by the tie and lifted him out the window into the night. They flew miles into the air. The wind was ice cold. Horatio stopped so high in the sky that the lights of city looked like mini pin-holes in the fabric of space.

"Now I want you to open that portal for me or you're as good as dead," Fat Kid screamed into George's face.

George blinked and started to giggle and laugh. He shook his head.

"No kid. That'll never happen, not ever," George said.

Horatio shook him and then dropped him.

George fell through the night sky feeling the frozen air coat his body. His thick dark hair shot back from his potato shaped face. His jutting chin was like an arrow head. George continued to laugh as he fell.

Horatio snatched George from death about a mile before impact. George was still laughing like a damned fool.

"Please, please, *please*!"

Horatio was crying now.

"How much are you willing to sacrifice, kid?"

George had stopped laughing for a minute and simply stared unfrightened into the boy's super hero eyes.

"What are you willing to sacrifice to save humanity?"

Horatio stared at the insane guy in front of him. The guy was much older than Fat Kid had originally taken him for back in the office. In the office he looked maybe forty, now he looked at least ten years older. The gravity of the truth in his face brought out the wisdom of the man. Horatio looked at him, deep into the man's face.

"Everything."

#

Dogg was back in Peko at The Clock Strikes Ten ghost hunter station. He was alone. He was always alone now except for Mel; of course she was gone now too. He had lied to Nick about the others. Mel and he were the only remaining members of The Clock Strikes Ten unit. When he heard the rain start pelting the windows outside, he realized that the end had finally come for him too. No career, no friends, and no family.

Looking around the station all he saw was a place that had once been filled with active enthusiastic friends and employees but now it was a pit of despair. He kind of wished that he had been stolen away just like old Tom. If he had then at least he would have had the opportunity to disappear.

When the doors opened and he stepped out into the rain not feeling a lick of the darkness that had once filled the streets he wondered what happened. Where had the black ecto cloud all gone? That ectoplasmic cloud was everywhere before but now it was gone, just like Mel was gone. Looking up into the sky he saw heavy rain drops splash down over his scruffy aged face and rain dowsed his cigar. He removed the dead cigar from his large lips and grinned a pitiful grin dropping the stogy into the gutter as he wandered off into the darkness hoping to disappear forever.

Stumbling into the gutter his eyes drenched in rain water and tears.

The headlights from an oncoming van hit him as he turned to face his own death at the grill of that speeding vehicle.

#

"Look, it's Dogg," Patty said pointing through the windshield as she slammed on the brakes.

"Dogg? Is Dogg there?" Mel's voice started to crackle and her transmission started to waver.

"Tam, we're losing her," Barb said.

The crackling of static filled the mic and then Mel's line went dead and another voice came across the line. It was a spooky voice, a dead man's voice. It was the GERMAN's voice and they all knew it.

"Dyin' times here."

The Death Strides all looked at one another as Dogg came running over to them. He was drenched in rain water now.

"How'd ya find me?"

"We didn't. We were just driving and you happened to step in our path," Barb said.

She turned back to Tammy.

"Tam did you get that signal triangulated?"

"I think so."

"Dogg get in here," Barb said.

Dogg blinked away some of the rain and pulled open the van door and slid in. This was his karmic reprieve.

"Guys, something is weird about where these transmissions are coming from," Tammy said.

"What do you mean?"

"The readings are all diverging on one spot," Tammy said.

Patty and Barb looked at each other.

"And?" Patty asked.

"It's Cobb Street. To be more specific it's coming from The Impossible Dreams Thrift Store."

They all looked at each other shocked.

#

George had directed Horatio not to the Dream Police offices but instead to the old thrift store on Cobb Street. They arrived just as the Death Strides' van screeched to a halt out in front of the store. When the ladies saw George Bokar they started to attack.

"Hold on. He's here to help us," Fat Kid said with his booming hero's voice.

"Help, like hell," Barb said and Patty spat on the ground in front of George.

He just glared back at them unperturbed.

"How's he supposed to help?" Patty asked.

"George, tell them," Fat Kid said.

"Let's get inside first," George said.

Horatio was still holding the front of George's tie and he led him inside the store like a dog on a leash. The Death Strides followed them inside. Dogg slid from the van watching this little encounter and then decided that he would take the cheap seats and watch from the rear. Better to be safe than sorry.

Once inside, Henry and Charlie Bokar raced to meet the group.

"Reinforcements!" Henry said.

"About time," Charlie snarled through his thick muzzle.

"Where's Nick?" Henry asked.

They all looked around.

"We last saw him at your offices. Did he leave with anyone?" Henry said.

Fat Kid had let George go and was now sitting on the sofa cradling Rachel's head in his hands.

"Who cares about Nick now? If he's back at my offices he's safe," George said as he was moving back behind the counter.

"What the heck are you doing, man? No one goes back there except Tom," Charlie said.

"If you're remotely interested in getting your old proprietor back from the brink you keep your mouth shut and pay attention," George said.

Charlie snarled at him but Henry held his undead hand on his brother's furry chest. They all watched George Bokar riffling through old cabinets and drawers, forgetting about Nick for the moment. George pulled jars and cans from various sources behind the counter and slammed them down on the glass surface.

"Now I'm not even going to begin to explain the details of what I am about to do. Suffice to say I am creating the potion for your buddy over there to save your friends."

Once George seemed to have all of his ingredients he squinted in the shop's dim lighting and spied a black cauldron on one of the shelves nearby.

"Hey, someone grab that cauldron there," George said snapping his fingers.

They all looked at the black pot on the shelf. Barb walked over and snagged it but was unable to lift it.

"Thing must be nailed down," Barb said trying to heft the cauldron again and again.

"Let me try," Charlie said skipping over on his werewolf legs. He reached out with his meaty paws but he too was unable to move the cauldron. He howled and snapped at the heavy object, but to no avail.

"I'll get it," Horatio said laying Rachel down.

He walked over and lifted the cauldron easily. He set it down gently on the counter top in front of George.

"Great," George grinned as he started dumping in the ingredients.

"More waiting," Charlie said grumbling.

Henry just nodded and slumped next to the sofa where Rachel began to stir. Fat Kid stood next to the counter opposite George as he continued creating his dimensional opening concoction.

"So how exactly does this potion, or whatever it is, help open the dimensional portal to this place The Keys To The Kingdom?"

Horatio was almost whispering now. He and George Bokar had struck a deal earlier to save Fat Kid's friends.

"You drink it kid. You will become the door into that dark realm. From the minute I saw you and you started talking like that hatchet was yours I knew that I had finally found our champion."

"What? Champion of what?"

"Light kid. You pulling that costume from old Tom's footlocker was like some cosmic neon sign – HERO, HERO, HERO! I bet the kids at school hate your guts, man," George said.

"What do you mean? I got friends," Horatio said defensively.

"Yeah right, those two Bokar Brothers. Some friends."

George stopped adding ingredients and then grabbed the ladle and started to mix the concoction. Fat Kid stared at this guy with his pointy chin and just felt like the strike to his ego had weakened him. He started thinking about his time at Harper

Elementary and now Barker Middle School and wondered if this stranger was correct. Was it possible the other kids made fun of him *because* he was actually a hero?

And then he looked at the nasty potion that George was finishing figuring that anyone willing to drink that slop and open themselves up as a portal to an evil dimension in order to save their friends had to have some hero's blood. He just prayed his blood would not be spilled in the process.

#

Mel sat in the leather swivel chair half asleep. She and Barb from the Death Strides had been talking and then someone she now knew as the GERMAN had interrupted them. After the shortwave went dead the reception with Barb didn't reoccur. Fish was asleep snoring as he leaned against the wall at her feet. Mel looked down at the red-headed goatee dude. She had seen Fish around and thought that he was kinda cute. Under the right situation she might have fancied him.

When the knock came on their door Mel jumped and ran to open it.

As she reached out to open the door Mel hesitated. Could the knocker be this GERMAN character?

"Hello?" Mel said through the door.

Fish stirred opening his eyes, wiping drool from his scruffy lips. He looked at Mel who was standing at the door.

"Open up," the voice said.

To Mel and Fish it sounded like a small boy. Fish approached the door too.

Mel looked at Fish who gave her the nod. She opened the door and in walked a small blonde-headed kid in a brown corduroy suit.

"What took you guys so long?" the boy asked as if he knew them.

"What took *us* so long? Who the heck are you kid?"

Fish looked down at the boy who stared up grinning. Fish and Mel stared at one another for a second and it wasn't until after the small kid removed a soggy cigar from behind his ear that Fish recognized him.

"Tom?"

The kid smiled as he lit the cigar. Mel stared, awed at the smoking seven-year-old.

"Fish, Mel, how long ya been here?"

Now they heard it. Tom's old gnarly voice, like broken glass across gravel, issued from the kid's lips making this surreal experience even more so.

"Did I fall down the rabbit hole and bump my head? You're old Tom from The Impossible Dreams thrift store?"

"Yes, my boy and we are late for dinner, so to speak. The others are back at the Dreams trying desperately to open a portal to get us all back. What they don't realize is that someone has been watching since the start, someone that's not my daughters," Tom said.

"Your daughters?" Mel asked.

"The Hatchet Sisters," Tom said regretfully.

"Are they here?"

"Yes and it's time they came home. Follow me," Tom said turning and leading them down the narrow corridor.

As they moved past the door two down from where they exited they heard laughing and drinking,

228

as if someone was having a party. It sounded like a horrible party that was out of control. Someone must have set a fire because Fish and Mel smelled burnt wiring.

"Tom, you said someone's been watching since the start, what did you mean by that?"

Mel was right behind the small boy. Tom didn't turn around. He continued down the corridor to a green pulsing exit sign.

"We'll talk about him, or *IT* later. Right now we need to regroup with the others at the Dreams. They can't open the portal door. If the GERMAN escapes into our world with the hatchet he'll kill every living soul on the planet," Tom said.

"The GERMAN? So he is real?"

"Oh yeah," Tom said reaching out to the exit door. "You two ready?"

"Is this GERMAN the IT you mentioned?"

"No time now," Tom said.

Fish looked at Mel, she looked back and pulled Fish to her. He grabbed hold of her too and they both took Tom's free hand.

"Let's go home."

They twisted the metal door handle and a spark of brilliant golden light shimmered in filling the corridor as they heard echoes of two male voices.

"Welcome back Tom," the voices said in all their ears as the light enveloped them and they disappeared.

Chapter Eleven

When Fish and Mel opened their eyes blinking away the incredibly bright golden light they were standing outside of an old rustic shack with a large radio dish sprouting from the slanted roof like a twisted bonsai tree. Glancing around Fish saw an endless field of white wheat. He tried clicking his jaw to make his ears worked but there didn't seem to be any sound here. Mel was doing the same thing.

Looking at the shack door Fish saw Tom the boy. He was standing at the front of the shack waiting.

"Tom, where are we?"

"MRBC," the boy said.

"MRBC?"

"Monkey Room behind the Closet, home of the Logos. We're waiting."

Tom hoisted up his corduroy trousers and adjusted the jacket fixing his blonde hair. Fish found himself straightening his own grungy attire. Mel didn't seem to care how she looked with the grease smears on her cheek and along her coveralls. Fish had to admire that brashness.

"Why are we here? We were supposed to get back to The Impossible Dreams," Mel said staring around the empty space.

"Not sure. These Logos fellas are kinda strange. Never really know why they do what they do," Tom said.

"THE BOY WHERE'S THE BOY?" A voice boomed from somewhere inside the rustic shack.

Mel and Fish grabbed for one another again and held on tight. Tom, the boy, wavered on his feet. The voice seemed to make the whole world shake.

"Duh, I'm here," Tom said.

He waved his hands in the air dancing about. Mel and Fish glanced at the boy but did not let go of each other.

Eventually, after what felt like an hour, when Mel and Fish let go of the other and plopped down on the white surface of the landscape exhausted by their quickly dripping away adrenaline, the door of the shack finally opened and two heads popped out.

"Hello," the dual heads said.

Fish blinked and saw that he was staring at two young men about his age, mid-twenties, at least that's what they looked like. Something beneath that façade pulsed like the wavering of a heated mirage. One moment they saw the young men in corduroy jackets, the next they saw eternity. Fish covered his eyes. He sensed that Mel was still staring at the Logos so he drew her into his arms directing her small face into his sunken chest. Fish was convinced that he stank like sweat but didn't care. Protecting Mel's sanity was more important.

"Hello, Logos...long time," Tom said.

Fish opened his eyes when he heard the adult guttural voice of old Tom. The proprietor of The Impossible Dreams stood in front of the young Logos, but he had changed from the small blonde-headed boy back to his old self. He still wore the rumpled brown corduroy suit and as Fish watched, the old man Tom placed his road ridden Fedora on his mangy old head.

"Yes Tom, very long. Care for a cheeseburger, cup of deep black GERKON?"

The Logos were two beings, clearly. One, the Logos Man, was bald with a round scruffy face, wearing dark square glasses and a yellow colored corduroy jacket. The second Logos, the Corduroy

King, had a thick patch of wavy brown hair sticking up along the top of his head, round dark frames and a slim face. His corduroy jacket was the color of caramel.

"Sorry fellas, but we're in a bit of hurry."

"You are always in a hurry, Tom," the Corduroy King said.

"Strange for such an old man, eh?" the Logos Man said.

"Very strange."

They both looked past Tom to his companions.

"This, this is Mel," the Corduroy King said.

"That's Fish. Look at his red goatee, ha! Where's Nick?" the Logos Man asked looking around.

"That doesn't matter right now. What matters is that the GERMAN is at work in DenMark. He has the Borden Hatchet..."

"Of course it matters. Every one of our creations matter," the Corduroy King said.

He seemed quite upset with Tom.

"The Borden Hatchet? Really, still living off Lizzie's fame I see. That hatchet is not Borden's. It's much older, much more unpredictable than being a simple device for evil. That young woman, Lizzie Borden had a dark heart. The hatchet was a reflection of that. Just like your daughters Tom. They too had dark hearts and you knew it," the Logos Man said.

"No, no that's not true at all. Michelle and Melissa were my angels."

"I'm sure you've convinced yourself of that over the years old friend, but the truth is once they took hold of that hatchet it wasn't the hatchet that turned them evil," the Corduroy King said.

Mel and Fish watched Tom's face crumble with anger and hatred for these eternal gods. How cruel they were.

"Stop it!"

Mel stepped forward pushing Fish aside.

"I won't let you talk that way to him. Tom's a good man..."

"No doubt," the Corduroy King said.

"You're the gods, yeah? Gods create things, everything. So you're as evil as his daughters. Are you responsible for that blackness escaping into our world?"

The Logos glanced at one another, smiling.

"Ah, young lady, no offense..."

"That's just about the time some idiot offends me," Mel said pulling out a wrench from her coveralls.

"We are neither good nor evil, but both. A cosmic balance has always been important for the survival of any creation. This blackness that you mention has over stepped its bounds, but we're not the ones to stop it. You are," the Logos Man said.

"Me?"

"Well, you'll do your part. The important thing is that the hatchet you spoke of finds itself in the correct hands," the Corduroy King said.

"And who's that?" Fish asked.

#

Fat Kid stood watching George finish mixing the potion that he would drink, allowing him to be the opening to The Keys To The Kingdom.

236

Henry and Charlie Bokar had left Rachel alone on the sofa and approached the counter as the time for Horatio to swallow the potion had come. All eyes, the Death Strides included, watched as the super hero stood waiting for George Bokar to complete the mixture.

"Okay, so that's everything. Next and finally I have a few words to say. Ah, you guys will probably not understand this because it's technically a language called HallAsian. Um, better to close your ears," George said.

They all saw the CEO's dire expression and wanted to refuse, but even Barb, the most rebellious of them, covered her ears.

As George closed his eyes and started to recite in the language that he called HallAsian, the small band looked to Horatio, still an eleven-year-old boy, buried in the massive muscle of the super hero suit. His large square jaw stood firm as he lifted the potion to his lips. George nodded and Fat Kid started to let the potion pour down his throat.

"NO!"

All eyes shifted to Rachel the girl. She had removed her vampire gown and stood watching Horatio drink the poison that could quite possibly kill him. Fat Kid saw her horrible, knowing expression and the remainder of the potion ran down his chin as he dropped the cauldron onto the wooden floor.

"AH!"

Horatio screamed in agonizing pain as the power of the potion surged like lightning through his veins. It struck his heart which stopped beating as they all saw the door to the dark, twisted Pole, The Keys To The Kingdom, emerge inside of him.

Someone screamed again and then the shop exploded in chaos with the small band running in terror as they saw Horatio Patterson being ripped apart in midair. Peering through this new portal opening was something pretending to be a man carrying the glowing Borden Hatchet. The bleak expression on this creature's face was even more horrific than seeing one of their friends torn asunder.

Outside, the rain still soaked the city streets. When Dogg heard the screams and saw the light shoot out from The Impossible Dreams he exited the van and sprinted to the shop. As he entered the thrift store he saw two things at the same time; one was the image of the GERMAN peering into our world from his dark Pole. The second image was of

Fish, Mel, and Tom emerging in the same space. It was as if two transparent sheets of film lay atop one another - Mel, Fish, and Tom on one, the GERMAN on the other. When the GERMAN saw the newcomers he withdrew. Dogg watched all of this in astonished horror. A second later the transparency that George Bokar's formula had created began to fill in. Mel, Fish, and Tom were tangible then standing inside The Impossible Dreams and the GERMAN was gone.

"Horatio!"

Rachel was on her feet grabbing Fat Kid as he stumbled and fell. His molecules had also miraculously replaced themselves.

"Rach?"

He whispered.

"I'm alive? How? I should be torn apart. The GERMAN? Where's the GERMAN?"

They all looked around. The portal was sealed up. The fabric of reality was closed but now they all saw a slight scar standing on the surface of reality like a string suspended in midair. They all stared back at George.

"I'm done here. The portal was open. You saw the face of your enemy. Now you will know him again when he appears to you," George said as he moved around the counter, past the tipped cauldron with the green potion dripping from it, and out the front door.

Dogg watched the CEO of the Dream Police disappear into the dark storm outside and did not bother to stop him.

"Where's the Borden Hatchet?" Tom asked sprinting to Horatio who had collapsed on the floor in Rachel's arms.

Rachel Brooks was the twelve-year-old girl again. Tom glanced around and saw the vampire gown on the floor next to the sofa and snatched it up. He dropped it on Rachel's lap next to Horatio who seemed to be hyperventilating now.

"Put on that gown girl, or else you're gonna die," Tom was shouting now.

All of their emotions were burning on edge. Charlie and Henry Bokar were staring out the open door with the rain blowing inside. Dogg was leaning on the counter for support. He was about to faint. He had seen some bizarre things in his ghost hunting times in DenMark but never as strange as what he saw emerge from that open portal. The evil that pulsed from the GERMAN was unmatched. Now the fabric of reality had been sewn up. As he watched the thin string-like scar in the space where the portal had been, Dogg noticed the scar heal itself and vanish.

"My god," Dogg removed his old baseball cap and made the sign of the cross over his chest. "Girl, do as old Tom say. Put on the gown - now."

The Death Strides stepped forward with Barb in the lead. She pushed old Tom and Dogg back away from the terrified girl.

"You watch your step, boys. That's a young *girl* you're bullying there. We don't take kindly to bullies. Ain't that right, girls?"

"That's the damned truth," Patty said crossing her arms over her slim breasts.

"I'm not threatening, I'm trying to..."

And then the whole world shook with the sound of a hatchet slamming against a log - over and over and over. The blade cutting away the veil of reality. When they saw the Borden Hatchet start to cut through the space where the scar had been a second ago, Horatio blinking back his pain lifted off of Rachel's lap.

"Horatio, no. You're too weak!"

"What's happening?" Henry shouted covering his undead ears. The sound of the hatchet was like a million screams.

"It's the GERMAN hacking back into our reality," a voice shouted from the front door.

Nick was standing there drenched. He looked angry and exhausted.

"Nick!" Fish shouted running to his old buddy.

Nick pushed Fish aside and moved into the inner area of The Impossible Dreams. He watched as the blade cut away at the fabric of reality in front of them. Charlie Bokar howled a mournful werewolf howl covering his mangy ears. His hairy muzzle was dripping with sweat.

"Nick?"

Fish stepped up to his friend and grabbed him by the arm. Nick was getting dangerously close to the inserting blade of the hatchet.

"We need to find the Brainbuster. I think it can close off this portal for good," Nick said staring at the hypnotic hatchet blade gleam in and out of reality.

"Brainbuster?" Charlie and Henry both said at the same time.

"I'm confused," Charlie said.

"The monkey stole the Brainbuster and vanished into the dark cloud. He still has it on the other side I think. If we can find it the ectoplasmic world that makes up The Keys To The Kingdom may finally be defeated," Nick said shaking rain water out of his eyes.

"But that means we need to have the GERMAN cut through. That's the only way we can get to the other side," Dogg said.

"If we do that we're all dead," Fish said.

"No, we're not. Horatio, listen to me," Tom said. "The Logos told us who our hero was, and it's you, boy. Only you can save our world from that crazy hatchet."

Fat Kid knew it. From the moment he saw the hatchet he knew that he was the only one who could genuinely wield it. Somehow Tom's daughters got their hands on it and it had not worked properly for them. Other national leaders, conquerors, presidents, dictators had tried to wield the hatchet but none had the spirit of Horatio Patterson – a hero's spirit.

They all watched Horatio as he stared down at Tom and the others. With his super hero suit he towered among the rest. He looked back at Rachel just once lifting her gown and kissing her on the lips.

"Put this on. Tom's right, without this magical protection you may die," he said.

"Why? What are you going to do?"

"I'm going to get that hatchet and end this once and for all."

Fat Kid lifted into the air hovering inches from the blade of the GERMAN as he continued to hack away at the wall of reality.

"Horatio, once you're over on the other side you need to look for my device. The monkey might still have it. You'll know it because it says RadioShack on it. If you can find it and activate it I believe that will close this ectoplasmic barrier for good," Nick said.

"Like ecto-glue?" Fat Kid asked.

"Exactly," Nick said.

"You're not going over alone," a deeply seductive voice whispered and all their eyes shifted to the beautiful but deadly vampire – Rachel Brooks, in all her night stalking glory.

"Rachel, it's too dangerous," Horatio said.

"You're too weak to go alone."

Tom and Dogg were watching as the fabric of reality was being ripped away like tissue paper now. The GERMAN's features were becoming visible. He would be through within seconds.

"Horatio there's no time to wait. You must fly through now before the GERMAN steps into our world. Now boy! Go!"

Horatio looked once more at The Impossible Dreams as his parents' faces flashed before his eyes. Henry and Charlie Bokar were watching him. Nick and Fish were standing nearby as were Tom and Dogg. The Death Strides were there too like some picture album of Coffin Kids – all of them returning for one last battle, and it was Horatio that would send the atomic strike. Finally he heard his father's voice saying – 'I love you Horatio. I always will.'

"Now!"

Fat Kid flew forward as the walls of reality tumbled next to the GERMAN. Rachel launched herself onto Horatio clutching his shoulders. He looked back at her for a second ready to scream for her to drop off but he saw the love and sacrifice on her face. Just before the evil being entered our reality, Horatio, always the hero, struck the beast and knocked him back. Unfortunately, with the forward momentum Rachel, Horatio, and the GERMAN went back through the portal and a cosmic explosion rattled the shop.

The portal opening was still there and it started to reverse its power sucking in everything around it like an event horizon.

"Get out of here!" Dogg screamed pushing the Bokar Brothers toward the front of the shop. They both battled against the black man, but the Death Strides saw which way the wind was blowing and helped carry Henry and Charlie Bokar out of the store.

"Nick dude, come on, this place is like going to implode," Fish said. He was holding Mel's hand now and she was dragging him to the front of the shop.

Nick hesitated for just a second praying that Horatio would return with the Brainbuster.

The gravitational pulled was massive. He felt his legs sliding out from beneath him now and knew without a shadow of a doubt that if he didn't leave then he would also be sucked into that dark portal.

"Nick?"

It wasn't Fish this time. Fish and Mel had left the store. Now above all the wind and rain Nick heard a single quiet voice whisper to his consciousness.

"Nick."

The young man turned and saw Tom, not as he knew him, an old man in a brown rumpled corduroy suit, but as Tom, the small blonde-headed boy of young. The boy that the evil cloud was searching for. Nick felt that perhaps all of this was simply a show, a staging. The GERMAN and the evil cloud didn't care about the hatchet and the walls of reality. There was something else flashing at him that he could not see.

"Nick, these thoughts are not your thoughts. You must go with the other Coffin Kids. This is what they want," Tom said.

"They who?" Nick screamed aloud now.

"The Logos," and with that Tom snapped his small fingers and Nick vanished.

#

They were through the twisting portal before Horatio was able to stop Rachel from grabbing onto him. She held him tight around the shoulders. The cosmic explosion that resulted in their crossing over the barrier between Earth and The Keys To The Kingdom made their entire existence quake. Fat Kid felt Rachel's thick long nails try to dig into his flesh like a frightened cat. As they flew forward into the darkness of the new realm Horatio tried desperately to keep his straight course. Now the only thing Fat Kid cared about was what the GERMAN held in his hand - the gleaming hatchet. He couldn't explain why. All Horatio knew was that he needed to have it.

As if Rachel and Horatio were forgotten the GERMAN turned his back on the newcomers and started off back into the darkness of the emptiness that surrounded them now. Even the thick glowing hatchet dragged along the ectoplasmic black surface of the ground as if the GERMAN had no more use of it.

Horatio watched the thing in human form begin to dissolve into the inkiness of the new landscape.

248

The area in which Rachel and Horatio floated was like some kind of a nightmare dreamscape where nothing seemed completely defined.

"Don't let go of me. I'm afraid that if we separate we'll never find our way out together," Fat Kid said.

Rachel, now in her full vampire regalia, clung to Horatio's massive muscled arm as they flew ahead.

"Where do you think that creep went? It's like he just disappeared," Rachel said.

"I saw him go this way. I need that hatchet."

"Why? What's so important about a hatchet?"

"I'm not sure, I just know that without that hatchet...something really bad will happen," Horatio said.

They flew ahead believing that they were moving in a straight line but the truth, unknown to our heroes, is that in The Keys To The Kingdom there are no straight lines, no order, or logic. That is its greatest strength and weakness. Rachel looked behind them as they flew forward.

"I'm really scared Horatio. I mean scared like I've never been before," Rachel held tighter to him.

"I know what you mean. This place is like a living, breathing toxic entity. It has a mind too. Can you feel it?"

"Yes, when it first took me I felt I saw its motivation, but now things are clouded," Rachel said.

"What's not clouded is that I need that hatchet. Once we have that..."

"Horatio look!"

Rachel pointed down below them. Now the area surrounding seemed to clear and what appeared to be a street formed beneath them. There was a street lamp, an old fashioned one, with a bench and two young girls.

"Those are Tom's daughters," Rachel said.

"The Hatchet Sisters."

"Don't call them that," Rachel said.

Horatio looked from the girls back to Rachel for a second. He saw hurt and anger in Rachel's beautiful green eyes. There was something emotional in her connection to these girls, Tom's daughters.

"Wait a minute, Horatio. Let's see if we can help them," Rachel said pulling away from Horatio.

"Rachel, no," Fat Kid whispered as Rachel flew down in a spiral pattern toward the young girls seated on the bench.

It was a scene from a picture postcard. Night, lit exclusively by the old iron street lamp, the girls looked like a pair of Grimm's fairytale characters huddled together against the darkness surrounding them.

"Girls," Rachel said.

It was as if they could not hear her speak. She flew lower, around and around until she was in reaching distance.

"Melissa, Michelle? My name's Rachel Brooks..."

When she was a foot from them the girls glanced up and seeing Rachel in her full vampire get up they screamed into the darkness. Their screams echoed back. Rachel flew away from them for a second.

"It's okay, really. I'm just a girl too, same as you," Rachel said trying to sound as normal as possible, but when she heard the slithering vampire voice she almost screamed herself. "Wait, wait."

Rachel held up her hands as she started to disrobe.

"Rachel, no!" Horatio shouted seeing her slip from her gown.

For just a split second Horatio saw Rachel's fully nude body without her gown. They both exchanged a glance. He quickly looked away feeling his flesh redden and when he looked back it was the twelve-year-old Rachel Brooks standing in her usual jeans and t-shirt. She was shivering the darkness.

"Hello. I'm Rachel Brooks," Rachel said.

This time the sisters did not withdraw. They stood their ground dressed in winter cloaks. They lifted their faces to Rachel and Rachel saw the most horribly demented expressions cross their perfect faces. The grins widened to expose emptiness like nothing Rachel had ever seen before. The Hatchet Sisters were not helpless creatures but clever predators.

Rachel saw their eyes glow with hopeful hunger as they approached her. She stumbled back falling over the bench.

"Ouch!"

Rachel struck her head on the black stones of the ground. She saw a quick flash of light and she was barely conscious.

"Welcome girl, welcome to our lair. We are the sisters of the hatchet, the sisters of eternity. Would you like to play with us?"

Their voices echoed in Rachel's mind.

"No, no I don't want to play with you not ever," Rachel whispered fighting the urge to succumb to the darkness around her.

She peered through her tear laced eyes and saw the sisters lift her vampire gown and toss it into the blackness of the realm where it disappeared.

"More magic, more power, power, strong life," they echoed one another as they approached Rachel.

When Horatio flew past them and snatched Rachel from the stones they howled like wild dogs robbed of their meat.

"No, Horatio, we have to save them. Tom..." Rachel tried to say more but without her vampire gown in this evil realm she quickly lost consciousness.

Horatio embraced her in his thick arms blowing heat from his body like an oven over her chilly flesh. Rachel relaxed but still remained unconscious.

"This was a big mistake."

He turned around and found that he didn't really know where he was and then his father's face surfaced in his mind again. This time he remembered an event at school, a recital that terrified him. Horatio did not want to sing in the recital. Some of the boys at school had made fun of him the day before when they saw Fat Kid and his father at the local goodwill store getting him some recital clothes.

Before going on stage he had suffered a severe panic attack, the likes of which he had never suffered before. He felt that same panic surge up inside of him now. Even wearing the super hero suit, George Bokar had been right. He was still just an eleven-year-old kid. When his father's voice came to him he remembered how his father had met him in the dressing room back stage of the recital hall. He had taken Horatio by the hands and had forced the boy to slow his breathing. Concentrate and control his breathing. His father said that he might not be able to control people's opinions of him but he could control his breath. Over and over his father had him recite a breathing chant. Hall, a single syllable. Hall, Hall, Hall...

"Hall, Hall, Hall..." Fat Kid began to recite as he closed his eyes.

In his mind one thing surfaced more than any other - the glowing hatchet. It was as though the glowing hatchet was calling to him. He saw the razor sharp blade gleam like a welcoming smile for him and only him. That steel smile mingled with Rachel Brook's beautiful smile and Fat Kid's eyes shot open. What he saw then made him also smile.

\#

The hurricane winds that had started with the GERMAN hacking open the scar in the portal wall began to lose its power until it was nothing at all. The Death Strides, Dogg, the Bokar Brothers, Nick and Tom all stood in the alley outside of Impossible Dreams and they watched as the store seemed to implode on itself. The structure still held but a torrent of dust shot out from the open front door shrouding them all in a thick coat of dust and ectoplasm.

"So that happened," Patty said spitting out dust.

Charlie was shaking off the black ectoplasm and dust like a wet dog but Henry seemed to like the gritty feel of it on his dead skin.

Barb was preening herself with a switch blade comb. They all looked horrible.

Dogg riffled through his pockets and pulled out a fresh cigar and lit it. He blew on it as he glanced over at Nick who stood staring back at The Impossible Dreams as if he was listening to something. Dogg stepped over to his young friend and gripped his shoulder.

"It's over Nick," Dogg said.

"Nick."

They both looked left and saw Mel and Fish approaching. They had exited the shop before the others and had missed the dust explosion. They were wet from the rain water but not a single bit of dust hit them. Lightning flashed across the sky and the rain continued to fall on them.

"Fish?"

Fish and Mel were walking hand in hand heading away from the chaotic scene.

"Look Nick, me and Mel were talking and…heck dude, we need some R and R."

"Meaning?"

"Meaning, we're splitsville man. Gonna go home and rest," Fish said taking Mel by the shoulders.

Nick started to laugh manically at his roommate.

"Same old Fish. When the chips are down you run off."

"Same old Fish? You kidding dude? Nah, this Fish is brand new. I'm the dude that just spent X amount of time in another dimension, *man*. I've been there and seen stuff I never wanta see again. Got it?"

Fish was in Nick's face now pointing him in the chest. They glared at each other as Mel pushed them apart. The others watched this interaction.

"Nick, forget about it. They closed that portal. Gig's over," Dogg said.

"Over, are you serious? Horatio and Rachel are on the other side. They sacrificed themselves for all of us. You guys don't have a clue about what they just did. Fish and Mel? Horatio was the first one to want to save you guys…"

"No one asked them to do that." Fish said.

"No one has to. That's what friends do, you idiot!"

Nick grabbed Fish and started to shake him. Fish pushed away and stumbled back.

They looked aside when they saw the Death Strides walking out of the alley toward their van. Nick sprinted to them. Even Charlie Bokar started to head off but Henry snagged him around the collar and drew him back.

"Where are you all going? This isn't over," Nick said as he reached the street.

"Nick, let them go," a voice - *Tom's voice?* - said in his head.

Nick glanced around expecting to see the old proprietor standing behind him but all he saw were the Bokar Bothers and Dogg. The others, Fish, Mel and the Death Strides had decided to desert them in their time of need.

"Nick, let them go. They have done enough. The portal is closed from this side. Horatio and Rachel are being tended to."

"What's that mean?"

Henry and Dogg were watching Nick talking to himself. They exchanged a concerned glance.

"Hey, Tom? Tom?"

"Nick kid, calm down. Old Tom's--," Dogg started to say and then noticed that Tom hadn't followed them from the Dreams.

The Death Strides were inside their van slamming the doors now. The CEO of the Dream Police Corporation, George Bokar, had exited The Impossible Dreams store shortly after he had completed his task of creating the potion that opened the initial portal. Fish and Mel had disappeared around the corner and probably drove off in Fish's Skeeter's Taxi Cab.

"Kid? Nick, you okay?"

Nick stood watching the Death Strides slam the doors. Barb leaned out her window and called to the remaining few Coffin Kids.

"My advice - pack it up, say your prayers, and never call us again. Let's go Pat," Barb said tapping the outside of her door with her fingerless leather gloves. Patty floored the van leaving about a mile of rubber on the street as the Death Strides disappeared down the block around the corner.

Nick looked back at Dogg who seemed really concerned about him and the Bokar Brothers who seemed anxious to leave themselves. It had been an exhausting journey but as far as Nick was concerned they weren't finished yet. George Bokar had said that his agents were combing the city to clean up the rest of the black ectoplasm, the portal to The Keys To The Kingdom was closed from this side, but there was something else that lurked in the back of Nick's mind, a feeling he had. *Something had been watching,* Tom had whispered in his ear. If IT wasn't the GERMAN then what was IT? Did IT want to come through like the GERMAN had originally tried?

"Nick? Why don't you come back to the station with old Dogg. We'll have a few drinks and forget all of this ever happened," Dogg said smiling.

"No, this isn't right. Something's changed."

Nick looked around.

"Tom, where's Tom? I need to speak with him."

Henry and Charlie just shrugged. The rain was still coating the streets. The neon Dragon signs for the Golden Dawn Chinese Restaurant blinked on and off.

"Man, I could go for some chow right now," Charlie said.

"Not wearing that mask you can't," Henry said.

Charlie elbowed Henry and Henry elbowed him back.

"The old Dogg could eat. What say you, Nick? Ya feel like a bit of the old Chinese?"

Nick was still looking around as if he had forgotten something. Brushing rain from his eyes he looked at the others who still stood on the street and then the flashing restaurant's lights caught his eye and he smiled.

"Sure guys. I could go for some Chinese. I'm starving too."

They all agreed that they were starving. After Henry removed his Civil War zombie cap and jacket and Charlie removed the werewolf mask everything seemed to be normal again. The rain had even stopped. Nick glanced back at The Impossible Dreams for just a second before they entered the Golden Dawn and saw old Tom locking the door. Nick's smile faltered but before he could think about that last image of Tom locking The Impossible Dreams, Dogg had him around the shoulders and was leading him inside the restaurant.

Chapter Twelve

The monkey, Roscoe, was playing with a small black box when the sisters saw him down the cobble stone street. They had missed the girl because of the bright-suited super hero. Roscoe was throwing the box into the air and then shrieked at it when the box did nothing. That monkey was horrible and Michelle and her sister knew that anything the monkey played with was dangerous. They had been here in this dark realm for far longer than they could imagine. Whenever the monkey came they hid.

This time though, the monkey seemed distracted by this box. The sisters noticed that the box looked as if it was made of some kind of metal with colorful buttons on it. How fun it would be to play with something like that. Their father had warned them about boxes and a girl named Pandora. She had played with the wrong box and let loose all the evils of the world. Looking around Michelle knew nothing more evil than this place. Perhaps she could get that box that so frustrated the monkey. She could put this evil place into a box and she and her sister Melissa could return home with their father.

"Melissa, look at the funny box," Michelle whispered as they stood several feet away from the monkey. They were safely tucked behind a wall watching the beast.

As Roscoe tossed the box and shrieked at the box the girls giggled. The monkey was scary but whenever something made it this frustrated it was time to celebrate. If only the girls could get the box.

"I want that box," Michelle said.

"No, I want that box," Melissa said.

Michelle scowled at her sister, but then rolled her eyes thinking.

"Maybe there is a way for both of us to play with the box."

"How, sister?" Melissa asked.

"The super hero. The one that frightened us. Perhaps he could get the box and give it to us?"

"Perhaps, that is a very good idea sister. But where is the hero?"

"Come," Michelle said leading her sister away.

#

He understood the catch-22 of this place now. Hall, the mantra that his father gave him, and what lay within that Pole enlightened him. Whether his father knew about the dimension called Hall with all of its grandeur or not Horatio couldn't say. What he did know is that his mantra while in this dark place had opened a window into a better place. That window into Hall, the one pristine world created by the Logos, was also a window into knowledge about all worlds or Poles created by the Logos duo.

Fat Kid smiled thinking about this dark realm's secret. The Keys To The Kingdom was a malleable Pole where, if harnessed, one could make their worst nightmare or greatest dreams come true. Because the place exuded darkness and despair most people immediately absorbed that feeling and the world fed off their fear. Horatio saw the truth of it. He wanted the hatchet more than anything else in this world. The hatchet was good. He wanted to save Rachel Brooks' life, and deep down he wanted to save the souls of Tom's daughters as well.

The first of these wants made itself manifest when he opened his eyes. The Borden Hatchet hung in midair before him. The effect was so startling that Fat Kid wasn't sure whether it was real or if he was dreaming. This question was solved when he reached out and snagged it. From the point of contact Horatio felt his strength grow ten-fold. His entire body alerted itself to the pulsing power of the hatchet. Where with others the hatchet absorbed their evil, with Horatio it absorbed his love.

"Horatio," Rachel said opening her eyes.

The corpse pale complexion that had coated her flesh had fallen away and now she looked like herself, better, radiant in his arms. Her green eyes flashed alert and alive. Before either of them said another word Horatio leaned down and kissed her soft lips. That was his second want.

"Horatio," she said.

"Come on we have one stop to make."

"And then what?"

"Then we go home for good." He smiled at her as they lifted into the air and flew off.

Rachel glanced over the landscape which felt less like a landscape and more like they were traveling inside a dark tunnel. There was no visible ceiling or floor as they flew ahead but they felt enclosed. Rachel had no idea where they were going but Horatio seemed to and that was enough for her.

When they saw what looked like a series of crooked buildings all pushed into one another and a glowing street lamp Horatio slowed. Looking down they saw the two young girls, Tom's daughters, running down the street. Horatio also noticed the monkey, Roscoe, one block over playing with a small black box. He used his telephoto vision to get a better view of the box. He saw the red RadioShack logo on its side.

"Nick," Horatio said and smiled. "Of course."

"What is it?"

"Let's gather the girls first and then I'll tell you," Horatio said.

"Gather the girls? But they're monsters. You saw last time."

"It's difficult to explain but trust me. I saw a window into another world, one that was filled with light and knowledge. I…please trust me."

"I trust you."

Rachel hugged Fat Kid as they flew down onto the black cobblestone street in front of the girls who stopped and shrieked in surprise.

"The superhero!" they both shouted.

Rachel cringed back when she saw their gleefully demented faces.

"Are you sure about this?"

"You said you trusted me." Horatio reminded her.

These creatures were worth saving? Rachel was ashamed at the thought of leaving Tom's daughters to this horrible place, but gosh, they were spooky with their dead expressions. They reminded her of animated marionettes.

Horatio flew down to them and settled on the black cobblestones. The lamp light reflected off his shiny suit. With his left hand on his wide hip and his chest thrown out he looked impenetrable. The large gleaming hatchet also helped complete the superhero persona.

"Ladies, if you would be so kind to climb aboard we'll get out of here," Horatio's voice boomed.

The girls looked at one another but then whispered to each other conspiratorially.

"Question," Michelle said raising her pale hand.

"Questions? Are you serious? We're gonna get you out of here, sister. Now let's go," Rachel said sounding more disgusted than she meant to.

"The box the monkey is playing with. Can we have it?"

Rachel and Fat Kid exchanged a concerned look as the idea of Pandora occurred to both of them now.

"That's a very dangerous weapon created by a friend of ours and I'm sure he would want it back," Horatio said.

"But we *want* it," the sisters hissed.

It took all of his patience to make Horatio not just grab the girls and exit The Keys To The Kingdom. He reminded himself that it wasn't the girls but the evil they had absorbed from this horrible place that caused them to be so monstrous.

"Just like you wanted my hatchet. Just like you'll want to stay in this realm even though it's a cancer that's eaten away at your soul. Your father's waiting for you on the other side," Horatio said and this caught the sisters' attention.

"Our father? Our father left us here so long ago, abandoned us to him…"

Stepping from the black folds of the realm was the GERMAN.

#

They were finishing up their Chinese buffet. Dogg had piled up six plates chock full of food. He wasn't kidding when he said that he was starving. The Bokar Brothers had eaten three plates a piece but Nick was pushing his Sweet and Sour chicken around on his plate. The whole scenario they found themselves in was just wrong, it didn't make any sense.

"Why are we here?" Nick said.

"Kid, Dogg's been askin' himself that very question for years," Dogg laughed, guzzling on a bottle of beer.

Charlie laughed at Nick and shook his head like maybe Nick was crazy. Henry differed in that he burped and wiped his mouth, but then looked at Nick.

"Why are we in this place or why are we on this planet?" Henry asked.

"Why are we eating Chinese food while Horatio and Rachel are still inside that dark plane?

Why don't you guys feel like helping them? And why do I keep hearing voices in my head?"

Now the Bokar Brothers did look at Nick like he was nuts.

"Hold on, kid. You hearin' voices?"

Nick nodded rubbing his bloodshot eyes.

"Damn, you gifted. They selected you," Dogg said.

"Them? Who?" Henry asked.

"Them Logos. Word I heard they's the puppet masters. We all their puppets." Dogg leaned back and struck a light on his cigar and sipped off his beer thinking on the Logos. "Was a time my brother Coffey say he worked fer them fellas, Tom too. See, they worked all kindsa strange missions and stuff. Their unit was named King Cobras. George Bokar was part of them too. Long time ago."

Dogg fell into a long silence.

"So what do they say, these Logos?" Charlie asked as he started picking at Nick's nearly full plate.

Henry elbowed his brother and Charlie pushed him back.

"They told me something about *leave it be*. Let The Death Strides, the Dream Police and the rest go home, they did what they had to do," Nick said.

"Well there you go. Spoken from the mouths of the gods. Now I'm definitely going home and crashing. You coming, Hank?" Charlie said sliding from the booth and snatching one piece of Nick's Sweet and Sour chicken.

Henry hesitated looking at Nick for a minute. The young guy looked totally heart-broken.

"Yeah, I'm coming. You covering this, Dogg?"

"I got it, kid," Dogg said finishing his beer.

Henry slid from the booth looking back at Nick and then followed his brother out of the restaurant.

"You know something else that's strange?" Nick asked Dogg.

"How much stranger can we get?"

"When you guys all turned to come in here I swear I saw old Tom locking up The Impossible Dreams."

"That is stranger considering that the front door blew off its hinges and the place was trashed from that explosion," Dogg said. "You sure you're not havin' flashbacks, kid? You know, maybe it was just a hopeful memory of seein' that old fool lock up before?"

"I don't know, maybe," Nick said looking even glummer.

"Tell ya what, I'm gonna pay da check and then you and me can check out the Dreams together."

"Yeah? Cool." Nick seemed to brighten up on that suggestion.

He actually took a couple of bites of his Sweet and Sour chicken and then slid out of the booth.

#

Tom had replaced the cauldron that George Bokar had used to open the original portal into The Keys To The Kingdom back on the counter top. The damn thing was heavy. Unfortunately for the old fella the physical world didn't allow for him to manipulate its space as easily as when he was in the other astral Poles. In order to stop the GERMAN he needed to create a concoction that he could use to permanently disable the beast. Call it a power drink to help boost his creative abilities. Killing a thing like the GERMAN was impossible. The creature, like the realm itself, was eternal. Once created it could never be uncreated. What Tom needed now was to make sure that the borders for The Keys To The Kingdom were welded shut. He couldn't depend on Horatio finding Nick's Brainbuster while on the other side. The Logos willing, either this potion would work or they would have to hold their breaths. Betting on the Logos was never a guarantee.

As Tom pulled bottles and canisters from the shelves to create his power drink he was struck with the image of his daughters' faces, how they had shined in the sunlight; how much his wife had sacrificed to bring them into the world.

"Melissa? Michelle?"

He felt them close now as if the membrane veil would be removed and his true babies would emerge. Tom had dreamed for years of reclaiming them from the darkness and moving to a small house in the country away from these horrible threats.

"Tom!"

When the voice came followed by the rapping on the front door Tom jumped knocking over some canisters. He stared straight ahead and saw Nick and Dogg watching him through the grimy window, a window that less than an hour earlier was blasted out, same with the front door which was back in place. Tom had that gift to repair minor things in the physical world. The shop had been put right as well, almost like new.

"Damn," he whispered, wiping his hands off on a handkerchief.

The old proprietor came around the counter and unlocked the front door. Nick opened it and sprinted through. Dogg hesitated looking at the repaired door. There wasn't a nick on the old frame.

"Incredible," he whispered.

"Get in here," Tom said and snagged Dogg around the arm dragging him through the door.

Tom slammed the door and locked it dropping the green shade.

"Why are you here?"

Tom barked moving back around the counter.

"Why are *we* here? Where the heck have *you* been? And why have you been speaking in my head?"

Tom looked up at Nick and then slammed his hand on the counter.

"Those Logos. They're meddling again," Tom said blowing his nose on the old handkerchief before sliding it into the back pocket of his slacks.

"That's a good thing ain't it?" Dogg said.

"Could be," Tom said as they watched him mix in some ingredients into the metal cauldron.

"What are you doing Tom?"

Nick stepped up to the counter.

"What's it look like? I'm *trying* to create the potion that'll give me the strength to incapacitate the GERMAN."

Tom was snarling now. He had measuring instruments and a cracked beaker on the counter.

"Is that even possible?"

"Logos willing," Tom said looking at the young man.

"You know, Tom, there might be another option. That monkey stole my Brainbuster device. If he still has it…"

"*It*!"

"What?"

"It! That thing's not a monkey," Tom said.

"Okay the IT stole my Brainbuster. If we could activate that device on the other side, that would theoretically close off that dark realm forever. Horatio knows about the Brainbuster. I told him before he went across. The Brainbuster has an ectoplasmic retract--"

"Okay kid, that's cool we believe ya. Tom, gotta plan to get inside that dark hole?" Dogg looked at old Tom.

Tom felt the fabric of the corduroy suit he was wearing and then looked at Dogg and Nick.

"Tough thing is when we're in the physical world there is only so much I can do. Now if I was in Hall, or the Monkey Room that'd be another story. I think though that I can create a power drink to help boost my creation abilities to maybe do just that," Tom said.

"Is it possible to travel to one of the other Poles?"

Tom and Dogg looked at Nick and they started laughing.

"Only by way of the Logos, kid," Dogg said.

Nick noticed that both Dogg and Tom were smoking cigars now.

"Well we can't just sit here mixing potions...can we?"

Nick wandered back and forth running his fingers through his growingly disheveled hair.

"Kid, things aren't as simple as just believing in them," Tom said.

"Why not? How do the Logos do that? Create?"

Tom stopped mixing the power drink potion and just stared at the long shot before him. He was kidding himself.

"Maybe this is a waste of time." Tom dropped the contents onto the floor catching Dogg and Nick by surprise.

He rolled over the counter like a young, sprite teenager.

"Come on! Come back to me! Teach me!" Tom was screaming into the space before him.

Nick and Dogg just watched the old geezer scream himself ragged.

"Tom, calm down. Yer gonna give yerself a heart attack, man."

Dogg was at Tom's side trying to stop him.

"Who ya callin' to anyway? The Logos ain't listenin' on this party line."

"The Logos are there," Nick said.

"It's always been a one way street with them," Tom cried. "They don't..."

"Take your calls," Dogg and Nick said, surprising each other.

Tom nodded his head, beaten.

"Maybe it's best to stop meddlin'. Maybe that's why them Logos ain't respondin'. If George was right about that deal he made with the GERMAN, those cracks you done opened, if they's closed, I mean really closed up, maybe we best let well enough alone," Dogg said.

"But we know that's not right. I mean, the GERMAN hacked away at our walls of reality. He almost walked through before Horatio knocked him back with Rachel attached," Nick said.

He looked at Dogg and Tom and then he sat down at the counter.

"If we're not going to save Rachel and Horatio then our only hope is for that *kid* to find and activate the Brainbuster, because thing is, we may have sealed off The Keys To The Kingdom on this side with that explosion, but the GERMAN is still over there with that hatchet, and if he wants in on our little blue globe than I'm convinced that only my Brainbuster and Horatio can stop him."

#

As the GERMAN stepped in from the folds of blackness Horatio automatically blocked Rachel. Fat Kid was holding the glowing hatchet in his hands and felt the pulsing power running through his body. Centuries of knowledge about this weapon coursed through his hero's veins. He knew that the hatchet was the key to destroying this seemingly insurmountable enemy. The window into Hall and the Logos' minds gave him that. It seemed like a strong Deus Ex Machina but Fat Kid had known that his entire life had built to this. Horatio felt complete. For the first time in his life he was the man he was meant to be. The suit and the hatchet were his super hero calling cards. Maybe if they lived through this he might even create a name for his super hero persona, Majestic Steele maybe.

"Horatio," Rachel said and he felt the chill in her flesh.

She was beginning to revert back to her frozen state from before. Horatio looked at the GERMAN, a simple looking man. Was he creating this change? Had he the power?

"No! Let her be!"

Horatio flew at the GERMAN who caught the super hero. The GERMAN's grip was like a vice. He lifted Horatio like a rag doll as the creature laughed at the boy's pathetic nature. Again Fat Kid was surprised at how the creature's face resembled his father's favorite actor, Stephen McHattie. His father? That brought his father back to him. The mantra Horatio, remember your mantra – Hall! Hall was ever at his call.

The beast pretending to be a man stood below him looking at the boy. Their eyes met and in that second glance Horatio understood the true key to this kingdom. The mind and the magic was all one needed to end this. To conquer, one had to control the mind, and the reality would be putty in your hands. Like finding the sisters in all this inky blackness would have been impossible unless he and Rachel hadn't...*wait a minute*.

"Rach, I think I know how we can..."

But when Horatio glanced down toward Rachel, the girl had vanished. A jolt of terror froze him.

"Gone, poof!"

The GERMAN whispered.

"Rachel! Rachel!"

Horatio looked all around but his love was definitely gone and he was in the grip of the enemy.

"What did you do with her?"

"Don't you know? Haven't you *mastered* my realm?"

The GERMAN stood watching Fat Kid. Horatio could see how pleased he was with himself.

"You bring her back. You do it now!"

Horatio raged feeling his eleven-year-old anxiety rush through him now. He was only a hero in the suit and he realized that. This creature before him with the familiar face was way out of his league. How did Fat Kid think that he could defeat this ancient creature? The whole time these thoughts flooded through his mind the GERMAN's deep grin grew deeper and creepier until his lips seemed to split his crusty old face. The more

282

Horatio looked at the creature the less human it seemed.

"Rachel," Fat Kid whispered in despair.

Remember your mantra kid. Don't be an idiot.

Horatio blinked at the sound of the Logos voice. He looked at the GERMAN who was now glaring up at him in triumph. The creature didn't seem to have heard the voice. If that was true it meant that there was a portion of his mind that was blocked to the GERMAN. If that was true then…

The GERMAN looked Horatio up and down as if sizing him up at a butcher shop. Would Fat Kid be devoured by this ancient creature? He was positive millions had died at the GERMAN's hands over the centuries. Was it possible that he would be just the same kind of victim? When the GERMAN reached out and tore off Horatio's super suit Fat Kid felt the arctic freeze of The Keys To The Kingdom surround him. Is this what Rachel had felt when she had removed her vampire gown?

"Puny magic," the GERMAN said dropping the colorful super hero suit into the inky blackness where it quickly vanished.

Horatio watched the suit disappear but instead of feeling terror and loss he realized that looking down he was the same super hero in size and power that he had been while wearing the colorful suit. How was that possible?

Remember your mantra kid.

The Logos voice echoed in his mind again.

Hall. Fat Kid whispered and he felt the spark of knowledge again. He noticed how the GERMAN was looking at him now. Horatio was still all buffed out with slabs of rock hard muscle and he was still holding the Borden Hatchet to boot. Did the creature know what he could do with that hatchet, how he could stop the GERMAN with one blow? Without thinking Horatio swung the hatchet and the blade glowed as bright as a sun in the darkness. The mirror metal reflected the GERMAN's true face and he screamed. When the razor sharp edge, an edge that could cut through reality, made contact with the GERMAN's skull two things happened.

First, Horatio's life flashed before his eyes. Buried thoughts and memories of his infancy became manifest. A thing lingered in the edge of his birth, his childhood, and now his preteens. The skeletal lips of the creature before him whispered a name into Horatio's mind. Second, he heard all the abducted souls in The Keys To The Kingdom sing out in glory as a brilliant golden light burst forward from the crack in the GERMAN's skull. Inside the light Horatio saw the truth of his own existence and the existence of everything; why the GERMAN did not just kill him, where Rachel had disappeared to and where she was now, why the ghost hunter groups had dropped the ball and stopped battling to save them. It was all clear inside the minds of the Logos.

And like flicking a switch Horatio saw one last image before he awoke on Earth. That image was of the hatchet blade, a blade that had for millennia spilled blood was now buried in the head of the GERMAN closing off the creature's obsession with the boy. Why so obsessed? Because the GERMAN and The Keys To The Kingdom were to crown Horatio from birth as the new figurehead for the dark realm. What the puppet masters from the Kingdom did not realize however was that Horatio Patterson was something special. He was a hero.

The secret whispered to Horatio from those skeletal lips was...Hall!

Chapter Thirteen

The day was like any other. Summer was ending and autumn was in the air. Horatio's father was home and he had promised his son a trip to the drive-in theater. It was Saturday, the last Saturday of the summer. Soon he would be back at Barker Middle School in sixth grade. He was hoping to see Rachel Brooks, that girl was a knock out. Every time Horatio saw Rachel his heart skipped a beat. Inside he always felt like they had shared something, but whenever he searched his memories the thoughts weren't there.

Horatio had wandered outside. It was a beautiful day. Blue skies and low eighties. The bees were buzzing. Horatio swiped at some dandelions blowing the cotton-like heads into the air. As he watched them float off his eyes noticed his father's hatchet stuck into the base of a tree stump. The boy walked over to the hatchet and touched the handle. Hatchet? Fat Kid ran the thoughts through his mind again, and again like Rachel Brooks, a hatchet rang a bell but nothing more. There was no logical memory associated with a hatchet.

"Hey son, careful there. That blade's razor sharp," his father said from behind him.

Horatio turned and saw his dad dressed in a checker shirt and blue jeans. He had cleaned up, looking forward to the night at the drive-ins. As he approached his son Horatio's father seemed to notice his son's mystified expression.

"Everything okay?"

Horatio looked from the hatchet to his father's kind face.

"Yeah...dad?"

"Yes."

"You ever forget stuff?"

"Sure. What kinda stuff?"

"Like memories, a kind of memory that you knew was really, really important but for some reason it was gone," Horatio said.

His father looked at him for a moment.

"Horatio, come have a seat."

His father led Horatio to their picnic table and they sat facing each other.

"Son, there are things in this life that will frighten you, things that might cause a man to shrink in fear. The mind is a very complex thing.

287

This memory thing wouldn't have anything to do with the coming school year would it?"

Horatio wasn't thinking about school at all. His memory loss was deeper than that. School was a fear he had but he quickly realized that his father might not understand how serious his fears about these memories were.

"Yeah I guess," Horatio whispered.

His father took Horatio's hands and smiled.

"Just remember to breathe and remember your mantra, Hall…Hall…Hall," his father said breathing deeply into his barrel chest.

"Hall?"

Horatio repeated his father's mantra and smiled.

#

Monday came and Horatio headed off to school after a hearty breakfast. He kissed his mother and hugged his father and then moved off down Gotham and Elm. Barker Middle School was just a couple of blocks away. He stopped at the alley that led to Cobb Street, a notorious short cut for all Harper Elementary and Barker Middle School students.

Something like a warning flashed in his mind as Horatio stopped and then glanced down the alley.

"Just shadows, that's all."

Horatio assured himself adjusting his back pack on his shoulders. He decided to go around the long way to school however. As he started back down Gotham he heard a voice calling to him.

"Well if it isn't Majestic Steele?"

Horatio turned on his heels and saw the Bokar Brothers, Charlie and Henry. They were smiling at him.

"Hey Chuck, Hank," Fat Kid said.

Horatio noticed how Henry, the dark-haired Bokar kid seemed to be eyeing him strangely.

"Majestic Steele in the flesh," Charlie laughed.

Henry elbowed him and Charlie elbowed his brother back.

"Majestic Steele?" Horatio asked not getting the joke.

"Yeah, you and the hatchet...ouch!"

Charlie shouted as Henry punched him. Charlie looked at his brother as Henry gave him a look as if to say *shut up idiot*.

"Oh, right. So where you headed?" Charlie asked rubbing his arm.

"School, you too?"

"Not today. We got some other junk to deal with first," Henry said.

"Turns?" Fat Kid asked, not exactly sure what that term meant.

The brothers looked at Horatio as if he had just told a nasty secret. Fat Kid didn't like their expressions.

"Okay, well maybe I'll see you guys around."

Horatio turned around and started back toward Barker Middle School. As he walked he glanced over his shoulder and saw the Bokars were still watching him and for some reason it creeped him out.

Later that day he saw Rachel Brooks sitting alone in the cafeteria. When he sat down next to her she looked at him like maybe he was a stranger, smiled and then excused herself. Some of the other kids giggled at him noticing the brush off. Horatio ate the rest of his lunch in silence. Same crap, different day…story of his life.

Epilogue

Tom sat on the porch of his small red brick home watching his girls playing in the field. Their hair was the color of summer wheat. The sun cast its ever warming glow down on them. It had been time to retire for years and now he had decided that this was the plot of space he wanted to create for his family. Horatio the boy had done it. Tom wasn't sure how, he couldn't see into the events of what transpired inside The Keys To The Kingdom, but he knew that Horatio, the hero, had ended it.

He smelled the apple pie in the oven. Rose, his wife, would be removing it in a minute and then they would all devour the sugary contents. The world he had envisioned was perfect, or nearly so. Tom had set up shop at 91 Greene, an address he knew better than Earth. When Horatio defeated the GERMAN Tom and all the souls that had been abducted by The Keys To The Kingdom had been restored to their normal states. Melissa, Michelle, and Rose were all returned. It was almost too good to be true. Of course like George Bokar had said there were always collateral damages. Horatio, the poor boy, would never know how important he was to saving all of their realities.

"Daddy come play," Michelle called from the lawn.

Tom smiled at his two angels and he heard Rose sliding the freshly baked apple pie onto the window sill.

"Girls, pie's done, come have some," Rose called through the open window.

Tom smiled as he swung slowly on the porch swing. His daughters laughed and frolicked racing one another to the porch. He was reminded of the Bokar twins. They would be watching The Impossible Dreams until Tom's return, if he decided to return. For now he was happy. The Keys To The Kingdom was closed, the ghost hunter teams were all alive and active in DenMark, Horatio, Rachel and the Bokar Brothers were alive and healthy. It was time to close this story.

"Tom, would you like a slice of pie?" Rose said smiling through the screen door.

Tom stood up no longer an old man but once again young. He stared at his wife through the screen door.

"I'd love a slice of pie," he said and opened the door kissing her in the process.

She kissed him back as their daughters raced past them into the kitchen where the pie aroma was intoxicating.

Tom looked back over his little patch of existence – 91 Greene, and smiled.

#

James Miles slept, finally. It had been weeks since he had really slept. Tonight something seemed to draw him deeply into what felt like an underwater slumber. The heavy layers of darkness covered him dragging him down like strong undercurrents. Someone stood in that darkness pulling him into a world of nightmares.

A being that looked very much like Horatio Patterson's father's favorite actor, Stephen McHattie, stood pulling the boy as if on a hook down into the depth of his vanquished realm. Horatio Patterson, the boy who would become Majestic Steele had defeated the being this round but the GERMAN was immortal. James saw this boy lurking on the fringe of the alley on Cobb Street where his younger sister Margie Miles was killed by the Hatchet Sisters. The boy longed for comfort, support, companionship. The GERMAN's deep set eyes and wrinkled skin twitched in a demented grin as he pulled the boy into his realm of nightmares. This boy would be his new salvation.

#

Somewhere in the bowels of The Keys To The Kingdom the monkey, Roscoe, was still holding the black box with the RadioShack logo on it. He wasn't able to make the stupid black box work. Roscoe was so frustrated he wanted to explode but when he heard the slithery whispery voice in his head, the one that told him to hand over the black box, he froze.

Something stood just out of sight. Roscoe felt its presence right next to him but no matter how hard he looked he couldn't see the speaker.

"My box," Roscoe scowled at the dark.

When the voice slithered again demanding the Brainbuster the monkey shrieked at the invisible intruder. Once the intruder stepped forward from the void Roscoe stopped shrieking and stood stark still. It was as if a serpent had struck him sinking a toxin into his bloodstream paralyzing the monkey's entire body, which went rigid. Roscoe's little furry hand held out the box for the intruder.

"Bad monkey. My box," the creature with the glowing lunatic eyes whispered to Roscoe.

The monkey did not want to release the box but he had no choice. The intruder was too strong. Roscoe had been in league with the GERMAN, a very powerful being, but this intruder was different – more slithery. It removed the box from Roscoe's frozen fingers and when its maniacal giggle started Roscoe shifted his eyes to see the cavernous open mouth with the layers of endless razor sharp teeth – teeth that had devoured worlds. He glanced up and saw the eyes again. As horrible as the leering fangs filling the grin was, it was the sunken glowing, knowing eyes that frightened the monkey even more.

"My box. My box. My lovely box," the intruder sang dementedly as it coddled the box in its small fragile looking arms.

Roscoe, the monkey that wasn't really a monkey, shivered with fear at this new creature before it. He didn't know what the thing with the box was. All Roscoe understood was that it was new, powerful, and hungry.

The End.

Printed in Dunstable, United Kingdom